KV-476-083

CONTENTS

ABOUT THIS BOOK   4

SECTION 1: INTRODUCTION   6

SECTION 2: GETTING IN TOUCH – THE BASICS   23

SECTION 3: QUESTIONS AND ANSWERS   45

SECTION 4: PHOTOCOPIABLE PROJECTS   52

SECTION 5: RECOMMENDED WEB SITES   88

SECTION 6: AT-A-GLANCE GUIDES   91

GLOSSARY   93

INDEX   96

ABOUT THIS BOOK

This book is a practical guide for Primary school teachers and those working with children writing, sending and receiving e-mails. It will help children get good practical use from using e-mail. It has been written by teachers with the help of Literacy and ICT educational advisors. It is a resource to help teachers use Information and Communication Technology (ICT) across the National Curriculum at Key Stage 2. Material is organised and explained in a practical way, using non-technical language. Where technical terms cannot be avoided, they are explained in the Glossary on pages 93–95.

If you are a Key Stage 2 classroom teacher, an ICT co-ordinator or newly-qualified, this book will show you how to use e-mail to communicate and share information, for research in lessons and for use in the classroom.

If you are a teacher with experience in ICT, then the practical projects in this book should be particularly useful. You will also find ideas to help you train and support less-experienced colleagues.

If you are a trainee teacher, you will find the practical classroom advice valuable as you build up your repertoire of teaching skills and expand your understanding.

If you are a parent who wants to take a more active educational role helping your children through the intricacies of e-mail, then this book will help you understand and support your child's teachers in promoting the best use of this communications tool.

Using E-Mail aims to show you how information exchange can be an important part of teaching and learning in schools. The book focuses on *Windows* PCs running *Outlook Express* e-mail software but can be used with Apple Macintosh or Research Machines computers running any proprietary e-mail software.

BOOKS TO MAKE SENSE OF THE INTERNET

At first, trying to get into cyberspace can be daunting. There is a lot of jargon, and the technology keeps changing. The basics, however, are not that difficult to grasp. *Using E-mail* is one of three ICT titles, produced by teachers for teachers, about making the best educational use of the Internet. Each title has more than 30 photocopiable activity sheets.

The other two titles are:
Finding Information Practical aspects of getting on the World Wide Web, searching for information and downloading text and graphics for educational projects.

Creating A Web Site Clear instructions and illustrated examples explaining how to build and manage a web site.

Internet Projects for Primary S

using E-mail

Michael Strachan and Frances Thomas

A & C BLACK

The authors: Michael Strachan and Frances Thomas are qualified teacher-trainers of Primary school teachers in the use of computers in schools.

Published 2001 by
A & C Black (Publishers) Limited
Alderman House
37 Soho Square
London WID 3QZ

ISBN 0-7136-5712-X

Copyright © A & C Black Publishers Ltd 2001

Acknowledgements
This book was produced for A & C Black by
Bender Richardson White, Uxbridge.

Project Editor: Lionel Bender
Designer: Malcolm Smythe
Art Editor: Ben White
Illustrations: Jim Robins
Production: Kim Richardson

Teachers' Notes and Photocopiable Activities created by: Lucy Poddington

Cover illustration: Charlotte Hard

Section 1: Introduction

The 'Introduction' contains background information about the Internet and e-mail, how they work and how to make the best educational use of the technology. There is also a summary of the Government's requirements for planning purposes.

Section 2: Getting in touch – The Basics

'Getting In Touch' provides a step-by-step guide to communicating with e-mails. There are diagrams, computer screen shots and a minimum of text. Many pages give practical hints and tips as well as curriculum guidance notes. The section includes features on sending and receiving e-mails, making an e-mail address book, and attaching text and image files to e-mails.

Section 3: Questions and Answers

This section answers some frequently-asked questions, such as 'What can go wrong?' and addresses security issues. It also describes the hardware and software you will need to send and receive e-mail messages.

Section 4: Photocopiable Projects

Photocopiable activity sheets provide teachers with activities for children to do in classroom groups or individually. These will help children to get the most out of sending and receiving e-mails.

At the start of the section are Teachers' Notes. These give ideas and suggestions for making the most of the activities. Most of the activity sheets end with a challenge, 'Next step', which reinforces and extends the children's learning and provides the teacher with an opportunity for assessment. These more challenging activities might be appropriate for only a few children. On some activity pages there is space for the children to complete the extension activities, but others will require a notebook or separate sheet.

The activities cover a wide range of curriculum subjects and are pitched at different learning levels. Some activities can be carried out away from the computer. Others are designed to be completed by using e-mail. The activities can also be carried out at home.

Section 5: Recommended Web sites

This part of the book lists recommended web sites and links to e-mail addresses that teachers have found especially useful.

Section 6: At-A-Glance Guides

Finally there is a checklist of basic computer skills you should develop and a glossary that can be photocopied and pinned up alongside your computers.

SECTION 1:
INTRODUCTION

➡ **What is E-mail?**   **7**

➡ **The Internet and E-mail**   **9**

➡ **The Internet, E-mail and the National Curriculum**   **11**

➡ **Using E-mail in the Classroom**   **14**

➡ **Linking Up to E-mail**   **16**

➡ **A Brief History of E-mail**   **21**

WHAT IS E-MAIL?

'E-mail' stands for electronic mail. It is a mechanism for sending and receiving information between computers linked together on a telephone or radio network. It is a digital alternative to communicating by the postal system.

Sending letters, postcards and parcels by post is so much a part of our lives that it is difficult to imagine life before the 'Penny Post' was set up in the early-nineteenth century. We take for granted writing letters and using ordinary mail to send and receive goods and gifts. From businesses to schools, relatives to friends, we depend on the mail to keep in touch.

The growth of the telephone and telegraph system during the twentieth century speeded up communications, enabling people to talk to each other all over the world. With the advent of the mobile phone, there has been another phenomenal growth in telephone usage and text messaging, which shows no sign of slowing down.

With the development of computers and the Internet, e-mail has become the essential way of sending typed messages from one computer to another anywhere in the world. E-mail has been around longer than other features of the Internet such as web sites. Now, every computer is a potential mailbox where messages can be opened or sent out. A decade ago, e-mail was mostly used by government agencies and academic circles. Now, it has become the essential communications medium for business, and a useful tool at home and in school.

WHAT ARE THE BENEFITS OF E-MAIL OVER THE POST?
E-mail has become popular because:
- it is quick and easy to use
- it is inexpensive
- it is very fast
- it is reliable
- it does not require a post person to deliver
- you do not have to go to the post office or mail box
- you can send many messages to many people, in one go
- you can store and file incoming and outgoing messages
- you can send and receive messages from almost any computer, anytime, anywhere
- you can send and receive e-mails on the latest mobile phones

E-mail uses telephone links and costs just the price of a local call. Not only can you send reminders, memos and letters by e-mail, you can also attach pictures and documents to an e-mail message. So e-mail is versatile, too.

HOW DOES E-MAIL WORK?

To send e-mail, a computer needs to be running an e-mail program (the software) and be linked to a modem and telephone line. A modem converts the digital signals computers use into pulses that can travel along the telephone system. E-mail software is usually supplied with computers or by the company that provides the Internet connection, called an Internet Service Provider (ISP).

Each person or organisation using e-mail has an address. An e-mail address is in two parts: a user name (or ID) and a domain name. The user name may be your own name or your school's name. The domain name identifies the organisation that looks after your mailbox, which is often your Internet Service Provider. To send an e-mail, you give it the receiver's address and 'post it' to your ISP via your modem and telephone line. The message is sent over the Internet to the receiver's ISP. There it is stored until the receiver links to the Internet and retrieves it.

The 'flow chart' below shows the movement of an e-mail message you send from your computer to your friend's computer over the Internet.

You type an e-mail on your computer and attach to it your friend's e-mail address.	Your message appears on your friend's computer.
The message is converted by your modem and sent via your telephone line to your ISP, which is connected to the Internet.	Your friend connects to his or her ISP and retrieves your message from the mailbox.
The message is stored on a 'server' at your ISP until it is ready to be sent.	The message is stored in your friend's 'mailbox' on his or her ISP's server.
The server interprets the e-mail address and passes on the message to a 'hub'.	The message passes through a series of hubs on the Internet to your friend's ISP.

THE INTERNET AND E-MAIL

The Internet is a worldwide group of computers made up of lots of smaller groups called networks. All these networks are connected by special computers called servers, and can share information using telephone lines, cable, modems and radio. The term 'Internet' really does express the fact that every part is connected and that messages can travel to every junction on the net.

The Internet provides two extremely useful functions: e-mail and and the World Wide Web. E-mail is a postal system; the 'Web' is a huge collection of information that can be accessed from any computer 24 hours a day. The information is stored at 'web sites', which are created by individuals and organisations on their computers.

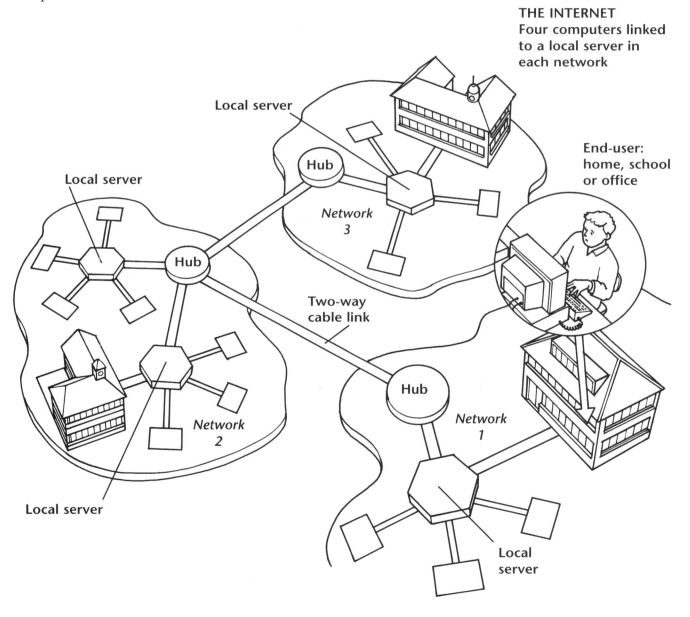

THE INTERNET
Four computers linked to a local server in each network

Local server

End-user: home, school or office

Local server

Hub

Network 3

Local server

Hub

Two-way cable link

Network 2

Hub

Network 1

Local server

Local server

Why is E-mail so Useful?

In theory, the Internet offers quick, simple and cheap access to people and information from around the globe. Browsing the Internet can be rewarding, fun and educational, but what makes e-mail so exciting is being able to attach 'multimedia' (images, movies, music, sounds, text and video) to messages and send them across the Internet.

Using the information-sharing capability of e-mail, children and adults can be talking to each other from different sides of the world, learning about new cultures and lifestyles and exchanging thoughts, opinions, experiences and photographs.

Sending and receiving e-mails via computer has become commonplace. Now, many e-mails can be sent and received using mobile phones, helping us keep in touch with family and friends and colleagues. We can send directions, greetings, reminders, jokes and gossip. So e-mail is becoming part of everyday life not only for business and commerce, but also for education and leisure.

Along with mobile phone developments there has been a dramatic increase in the amount of information that can be transported over the Internet using copper telephone wiring. This has been achieved by expanding the 'bandwidth' of signals – effectively allowing more information to pass per second without increasing the thickness of the wires (in the same way that more water flows from a faucet as the tap is opened more). An increasing number of companies and institutions are using broadband technologies to increase the line capacity and send large video and audio files attached to e-mails to suitably equipped clients.

Broadband is a development that particularly suits the cable companies. For homes that have cable TV, it is good investment to combine the cost of TV, telephone and Internet access charges in a single cable package. As more and more homes get 'wired up' to cable, so e-mail is likely to become the standard communications system.

THE INTERNET, E-MAIL AND THE NATIONAL CURRICULUM

Using the Internet is part of Information and Communication Technology (ICT), which is a foundation subject in the National Curriculum. This means it is expected to be at the heart of the educational process and used wherever it is appropriate and helpful. Using e-mail is an integral part of this plan.

Much of the curriculum information from the Department for Education and Employment (DfEE) and the Qualifications and Curriculum Authority (QCA) is already online.

You can visit the DfEE and QCA web sites at:
www.dfee.gov.uk
www.qca.org.uk

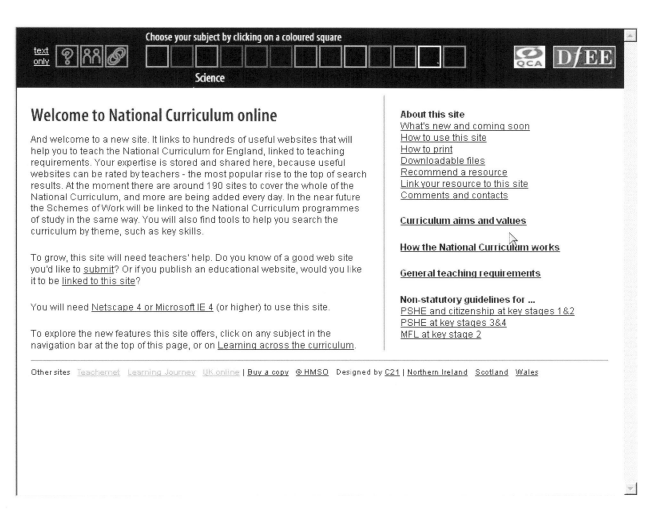

On the next page is the statement of the Information and Communication Technology requirements for Key Stage 2. The statements most relevant to e-mail are underlined.

The ICT requirements for Key Stage 2 Unit 3E state that:

'In this unit children learn to use e-mail (electronic mail) to send and receive messages. They learn about communicating over distances and will need to consider and compare different methods of communication.

Using e-mail can help children develop their reading and writing skills and develop their knowledge of the wider community. The unit requires collaboration with other schools.

Children will apply what they have learnt in this unit when using e-mail, gathering information, developing collaborative projects, and writing for other audiences.'

These requirements are divided into five areas:
1. Knowledge, skills and understanding
2. Developing ideas and making things happen
3. Exchanging and sharing information
4. Reviewing, modifying and evaluating work as it progresses
5. Breadth of study

[Below, topics related specifically to e-mail are underlined.]

1. Knowledge, skills and understanding
PUPILS SHOULD BE TAUGHT:
a   to talk about what information they need and how they can find and use it (for example, searching the Internet or a CD-ROM, using printed material, asking people);
b   how to prepare information for development using ICT, including selecting suitable sources, finding information, classifying it and checking it for accuracy (for example, finding information from books or newspapers, creating a class database, classifying by characteristics and purposes, checking the spelling of names is consistent);
c   to interpret information, to check it is relevant and reasonable and to think about what might happen if there were any errors or omissions.

2. Developing ideas and making things happen
PUPILS SHOULD BE TAUGHT:
a   how to develop and refine ideas by bringing together, organising and reorganising text, tables, images and sound as appropriate (for example, desktop publishing, multimedia presentations);

b how to create, test, improve and refine sequences of instructions to make things happen and to monitor events and respond to them (for example, monitoring changes in temperature, detecting light levels and turning on a light);

c to use simulations and explore models in order to answer 'What if . . .?' questions, to investigate and evaluate the effect of changing values and to identify patterns and relationships (for example, simulation software, spreadsheet models).

3. Exchanging and sharing information

PUPILS SHOULD BE TAUGHT:

a how to share and exchange information in a variety of forms, including e-mail (for example, displays, posters, animations, musical compositions);

b to be sensitive to the needs of the audience and think carefully about the content and quality when communicating information (for example, work for presentation to other pupils, writing for parents, publishing on the Internet).

4. Reviewing, modifying and evaluating work as it progresses

PUPILS SHOULD BE TAUGHT TO:

a review what they and others have done to help them develop their ideas;

b describe and talk about the effectiveness of their work with ICT, comparing it with other methods and considering the effect it has on others (for example, the impact made by a desktop-published newsletter or poster);

c talk about how they could improve future work.

5. Breadth of study

DURING THE KEY STAGE, PUPILS SHOULD BE TAUGHT THE KNOWLEDGE, SKILLS AND UNDERSTANDING THROUGH:

a working with a range of information to consider its characteristics and purposes (for example, collecting factual data from the Internet and a class survey to compare the findings);

b working with others to explore a variety of information sources and ICT tools (for example, searching the Internet for information about a different part of the world, designing textile patterns using graphics software, using ICT tools to capture and change sounds);

c investigating and comparing the uses of ICT inside and outside school.

USING E-MAIL IN THE CLASSROOM

The Internet and e-mail link all of us to vast databases of information. They allow us to visit and communicate with people, places and organisations all over the world. In education, e-mail enables collaborative projects between classes within a school and between widely separated schools. Even if schools are separated by different time zones, e-mails can be sent to wait until the receiver is ready to open them. With e-mail, you can open, answer and send messages at your convenience. By setting up an address book with contact groups, the same e-mail can be sent to several people or to several classes or schools at the same time.

By learning to use e-mail responsibly, children can be taught to consider the different purposes and audiences for whom e-mail is appropriate. For example, children can communicate directly with each other to share ideas and experiences. This turns e-mail into a diary or penpal form. E-mail can also be used to collect and send information and data for class projects in a range of subjects, for example, comparing lifestyles and environmental features, weather, economic factors, historical developments, and so on. The information can be downloaded from web sites on the Internet, copied from CD-ROMs or imported from digital cameras or scanners.

A GUIDING, HANDS-ON APPROACH

People learn best from other people and not from machines. It is in the supportive environment of a well-organised Primary classroom or home that children can try out ideas and begin to structure their knowledge. Using e-mail has a crucial role to play in teaching Information and Communication Technology to young learners, but this experience needs to be guided and supported.

Below are examples of ways in which you can use e-mail. For each of the areas listed, you will find web site addresses listed in Section 5. Most of the these web sites have 'Contact us' options that allow you to submit questions and receive answers and information via e-mail.

KEEPING UP-TO-DATE ONLINE

Children and teachers can use e-mail to keep up-to-date with and exchange any kind of information obtained from web sites, whether it is fun or informative or both, for example news, fashion, gossip, music, puzzles or advice.

QUESTION THE EXPERTS

If you and your pupils know where to go, you can find an expert on just about any subject. Increasingly, the educational content of the Internet is including e-mail real-time links to specialists and experts. That means that it is possible to ask an expert a question and receive an answer almost immediately.

VIRTUAL MUSEUMS AND GALLERIES

E-mail can be used to ask museum experts specific questions relating to permanent exhibitions and exhibitors. Many museums also offer an e-mail postcard system so that you send someone a picture from the exhibition as part of an educational project.

TEACHER TRAINING

In most cases, Government and ICT training initiatives involve some face-to-face sessions with experienced trainers, but it also depends on continuing support and advice being provided via e-mail. This makes e-mail a feature of teacher training at all levels, whether provided by LEAs and Government agencies or by commercial enterprises.

SEN RESOURCES AND INFORMATION

There are organisations that specialise in providing e-mail communication and information for parents and teachers of children with every kind of Special Educational Need.

ANNOUNCEMENT AND CHAT LISTS

E-mail is used by various organisations and groups of people to send out regular bulletins of information. Teachers and pupils can join these 'mailing lists' to receive up-to-date information about local museums, library events and so on. Chat lists are discussion groups. Members send messages to the group and they are forwarded to all the other members. Chat lists are ideal for exchanging information between classes or between schools.

GREETINGS, BIRTHDAY AND FESTIVAL CARDS

There are several web sites that allow you to choose an e-mail card, add a personal message and send the card to a relative or friend anywhere in the world – at no cost. The card company will e-mail you to confirm the card has been sent and received. This is a good way of keeping in touch with 'pen pals' and to support work on how people of different faiths and cultures celebrate festivals and events at different times in their lives.

THE FUTURE OF THE INTERNET AND E-MAIL IN EDUCATION

If you and your pupils have access to laptop computers or hand-held computing devices, these can be connected into the school network. Many people can then use e-mail together or in their own time. Some forecasters suggest that this is the future for computer-use in education. They foresee that every child will be equipped with her or his own laptop to be used at home and at school. The Internet and e-mail will then become the main links between home and school as well as between schools and their LEAs and Government agencies.

LINKING UP TO E-MAIL

Most Primary schools and the majority of homes are equipped with stand-alone computers, that is, computers that are not linked by cables to any other computer. However, an increasing number of schools are networked. This means that one machine acts as a server (host). The host computer is connected all the time to the Internet. It stores and relays the software and web site information to the other computers in the network. The diagram below shows the principles of a school computer network.
Either type of set-up is ideal for using e-mail.

A SIMPLE CABLE NETWORK

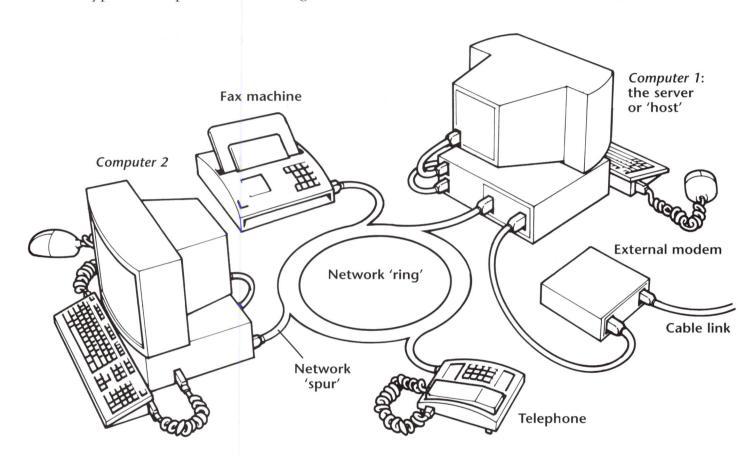

Fax machine

Computer 2

Computer 1:
**the server
or 'host'**

Network 'ring'

Network
'spur'

External modem

Cable link

Telephone

DIFFERENT SORTS OF E-MAIL

There are two main types of e-mail: one supplied by your Internet Service Provider and one that is web-based. If you are working on a stand-alone computer, at school or at home, your specific computer and its e-mail software are connected to the Internet by an Internet Service Provider (ISP), such as your local cable company. The ISP will provide you with your e-mail access, username and password. Similarly, computers on a network at school will have e-mail access via the company that set up and installed the system. With computer-based e-mail, your 'inbox', 'outbox' and address book are stored on your computer.

With a web-based e-mail system, such as *Hotmail* or *ePALS*, you can send and receive e-mail from any computer, anywhere, at any time. You get access to the Internet via a web site, then key in your e-mail address and password to send and receive messages. Here, your inbox and outbox are stored remotely, on a web site, and you do not have a stored address book.

The advantage of web-based mail is that you can send and receive messages on the move, for example from an office using a laptop computer or from an Internet café on the High Street. However, with some web-mail accounts, you cannot send attachments and there is a limit on the size of messages you can send and receive.

ISP E-MAIL SYSTEM

Your computer

Inbox   Message store   Outbox

Address Book

ISP 'server'

Your mailbox

E-mail from the Internet   to the Internet

WEB-MAIL SYSTEM

Any computer

Inbox   Outbox

Web site   To the Internet

Single mailbox shared by everyone

E-mail from the Internet

17

INTERNET SERVICE PROVIDERS

As teachers, you will be linked to the Internet by an Internet Service Provider (ISP). There may come a time when you need to sign up with your own choice of ISP. Online services such as *America OnLine (AOL)* and *CompuServe* connect you to the Internet and provide plenty of their own content, including chat rooms and messenger services where you can talk with like-minded people – hopefully in a filtered environment.

All the big ISPs offer these services, but teachers and parents may prefer to use the dedicated and protected areas maintained by organisations such as *Epals* or *Think.com,* or simply stick to e-mail. Most of the smaller ISP companies provide very little original content. You just use their services for e-mail or to venture out on to the Web and find what interests you.

Here are some questions to consider when choosing an ISP. Remember, even connection services that appear to be free may have hidden costs.

- Is there a monthly fee or subscription?

- Is there an affordable annual charge?

- Are there extra charges for being online?

- Does the company provide a CD-ROM with preconfigured connection software for your computer?

- Is there readily available, free telephone support?

GETTING STARTED

Before venturing into e-mail, you need to be comfortable with some basic computer 'household management'. You need:

- word-processing skills

- mouse and keyboard skills

- the ability to save, organise and manage files.

You will find a basic checklist of computer skills in Section 6. Work through this list and practise the skills until you are confident.

An E-mail Health Warning

E-mail is one of the most exciting and fast-developing aspects of the Internet. There are, however, problems as well as possibilities. In the home and school, e-mail is open to abuse by unscrupulous individuals, groups and companies who wish to target young and impressionable people. The best safeguard is to use a filtered or monitored access to the Internet provided by reputable Internet Service Providers.

A further safeguard is to develop and sustain children's critical awareness of the quality and motivation behind the e-mails and attachments they may receive.

For web-mail it is essential that teachers use and recommend only web sites and organisations that guarantee a filtered, monitored and secure e-mail service. Two examples are *ePALS.com Classroom Exchange* and *Think.com*. With these, teachers can set up secure accounts for children which they can monitor and control with a guarantee that every effort is being made to ensure the privacy and safety of children and teachers.

Below are guidelines for using e-mail safely in the classroom. Make these part of your lesson plans.

E-mail Alert for Adults

WHAT TO DO IF YOU WANT TO PROTECT AGAINST SUSPICIOUS E-MAIL:
- Always use a filtered, monitored system for yourself and children in your care.
- Never respond to messages that are suggestive, obscene, threatening or that make you feel uncomfortable.
- Never give out any personal information (such as addresses or phone numbers) to anyone you have not personally verified.

WHAT TO DO IF YOU RECEIVE A SUSPICIOUS E-MAIL:
- Don't open any attachments – they may contain a virus or unpleasant images.
- If the e-mail comes from another school or an organisation's web site, make a note of the return URL and get someone you trust to verify that the individual who sent it is a staff member.
- If the school or organisation does not have a web site, check with the appropriate LEA or call directory assistance to find out if the school or group exists and get someone you trust to verify the identity of the individual.

E-mail Alert for Pupils

HOW TO AVOID SUSPICIOUS E-MAIL:
- Always use the e-mail system recommended by your parents, teachers or guardians.
- Never answer messages that are suggestive, obscene, threatening or that make you feel uncomfortable.
- Never give out any personal information (such as addresses or phone numbers) to anyone you don't know. If in doubt, talk to your parents, teachers or guardians.

WHAT TO DO IF YOU RECEIVE A SUSPICIOUS E-MAIL:
- Never arrange a face-to-face meeting without a parent, teacher or guardian present.
- Always let a teacher, parent or other trusted adult know if you receive a suspicious or unpleasant e-mail message.

GOING IT ALONE

If you have not yet got your own computer, here are some guidelines to help you choose the ideal machine for browsing the net and using e-mail. First, you need to decide whether to buy a *Windows* PC or an *Apple Macintosh*. It is best to have the same type of computer at home as you or your children use at school.

1 Talk to friends and colleagues who have recently bought machines and get their views, particularly on the help and support offered as part of the package. Then visit the computer stores and look at the demonstrations to compare the range of machines on offer. Take a knowledgeable friend with you.

2 Look for a PC or *Apple* machine with a modem and the largest hard disk you can afford. The hard disk is where you store programs and the files you create. It needs to be at least 4 Gigabytes.

3 You also need short-term memory power called random-access memory (RAM) – at least 64 Mb. You need 128 Mb RAM to deal with big image, video or DVD files that can be attached to e-mails.

4 An Internet Service Provider (ISP) should provide the affordable link to the Internet. Networked schools will have been contracted with an ISP during purchase and installation. Individuals may find this already set up on the computer they buy. Find out about an ISP before committing yourself to using them. Check that your ISP allows web-mail.

5 The support contract and guarantee are crucial. Having someone who will visit your home to sort out problems is invaluable, whereas a telephone hotline may cause frustration. Make sure your support contract covers your e-mail system.

6 A good laser or inkjet printer is important. Many computer offers now come with the printer bundled in. If you are choosing a printer separately, check how much the ink cartridges will cost, to avoid too much ongoing expenditure, and find out how many pages per minute the machine prints to avoid delays.

7 Scanners and digital cameras are fun and, if they come as part of the package, you will certainly find many uses for them. For example, if you take pictures of your class on an educational visit, you can put the photographs straight on to the computer network or attach them to your e-mails. You can also scan postcards or other souvenirs of the trip and attach these.

8 If e-mail software is not pre-installed on your machine, you will have to load it from a CD supplied by your ISP. Follow the instructions that appear on your computer screen. You will be asked to choose an e-mail address and register a password. Most ISPs allow you to have several e-mail addresses.

HINTS AND TIPS

If you are buying your own equipment make sure you have an on-site support contract.

Get at least a 17" monitor, for an easier display.

Choose a computer that has as much hard disk capacity (RAM) as you can afford.

TECHNICAL NOTES

The processor is the microchip at the heart of any computer. The speed at which it processes information is measured in megahertz (MHz). The higher the number, the faster the computer goes. Your computer needs at least 600 MHz to give you a fast e-mail service.

An internal modem is the box that connects you to the Internet. The speed at which the modem connects you is measured in kilobytes per second (Kbps) – the faster the connection, the better.

A Brief History of E-mail

It is difficult now to imagine a world without the Internet and e-mail. Yet only a few years ago, we relied solely on books, radio, film, television and tape recorders to provide children with an exciting outlook on the changing world. Also, until the advent of e-mail, it was difficult and rare for teachers and pupils in one school to communicate from the classroom with colleagues and friends in another school.

Like so many ground-breaking technologies, computers and the Internet were conceived in time of war. During World War II, the Enigma code-breakers at Bletchley Park in England never imagined that, in their lifetimes, the computer systems they developed to solve numerical codes would shrink from their house-sized machines to tiny accessories.

Worldwide Networks

The Cold War of the 1960s was the driving force that saw smaller desktop computers becoming common in universities and research institutions in the United States. The idea of a global network of computers was proposed by US research organisations in 1962, and by 1965 a Massachusetts computer was connected successfully to one in California over the telephone line.

It made military sense for the US Government and its key agencies, university departments, research companies and others to be connected electronically by adaptable networks. It was thought that, in the event of attack, enough of the system of government would survive and, hopefully, important messages could still be transmitted and vital records protected.

This system, known as ARPANET (Air Raid Precaution Advanced Network), was brought online in 1969. In the following years many other universities and government contractors joined in the new network. In 1971, the first e-mail messages were sent between these pioneering organisations. So far, the United States had taken the lead but this was to change.

Everyday Computers

It was in 1989 that the initiative returned to Europe. Desktop computers were becoming more powerful and now had a host of new user-friendly features, such as a graphical interface (a display screen with clickable pictures), a mouse for moving around a pointer on the screen, and more storage memory. Instead of having to type in lines of complicated code, even a newcomer could point a mouse to an onscreen picture called an icon and click a button to send instructions or save data for later retrieval.

As computers became part of school and home life, devising software to run on them grew into a multi-million pound industry. The Internet, however, was still just a network of smaller networks and its coverage was not worldwide. There was no standard or systematic way of connecting all the bits of information and messages flying around with all their destinations.

DATA-SWAPPING

Throughout this period, scientists had always been at the forefront of computer development. At the research laboratories of CERN (European Organisation for Nuclear Research), the foundations for the World Wide Web were being laid. All of the projects, researchers and computers at CERN needed a way of swapping information freely, so that new developments and finds could be accessible to all. The researchers needed to exchange ideas and results quickly and cheaply.

Scientist, Tim Berners-Lee, and others at CERN established that the computers needed to be speaking the same language, or electronic communication would be chaos. The language they devised is now called TCP/IP (Transmission Control Protocol, or Internet Protocol), and it ensures that data sent from one computer to another is dealt with in a special way. All data, whether it is e-mail, sounds or images, is broken down into 'packets'. Each packet is tagged with an 'address' – coded information about its point of origin and its destination. When the packets arrive, they are assembled in the right place and in the right order. All this is done in fractions of a second and no one really notices anything unless something goes seriously wrong.

With a standard address system established, huge corporations such as Microsoft realised the enormous commercial and educational potential of a worldwide system of computer communications. They were the driving force in establishing the World Wide Web and e-mail. The motivation for the subsequent phenomenal growth of the Internet, which shows little sign of slowing down, has come from millions of individuals and companies, large and small, that have realised its potential as a communicating tool. E-mail, discussion boards and chat lines have proliferated and can be found in every commercial enterprise and every academic institution. They are also destined to be part of every school and classroom.

SECTION 2:
GETTING IN TOUCH – THE BASICS

GETTING STARTED | Setting up an E-mail account | 24
| Starting up on a stand-alone PC | 25
| Starting up on a network PC | 27
| Starting up on an Apple Mac | 28
| Starting 'Outlook Express' | 29
| 'Outlook Express' main window and panels | 30
| 'Outlook Express' toolbar | 31

READING MAILS | Receiving e-mails . . . | 32
| . . . and Reading e-mails | 33
| To print a message | 33

WRITING E-MAILS | Writing a new message | 34
| Addresses and Writing Style | 35
| Netiquette (or good e-mail manners) | 35

ADDRESS BOOK | Setting up an Address Book | 36
| Adding new Addresses manually | 37
| Creating Address Groups | 38
| Adding contacts to a group | 38

REPLYING AND FORWARDING | Replying to messages | 39
| Forwarding and carbon copying | 39
| Managing your e-mail 1 | 40
| Managing your e-mail 2 | 41
| Attachments | 42
| How to handle attachments | 43

ISSUES | Newsgroups and Chatrooms | 44

Setting up an E-mail Account

If you work mainly on a school network, then your details have already been entered into the system by the network manager or ICT Co-ordinator and you will have a 'username' and 'password'.

If you have signed up with an ISP or Access Provider, you will receive a CD from them containing the Internet connection software, and your username or registration number and password will probably come separately for security reasons. Then follow the steps below.

1 Close down any programs running on your computer and insert the CD.

2 The installation process should begin automatically with instruction boxes appearing on screen. Insert your username or registration number and password when prompted.

3 If you are asked to insert your own username, think carefully as it forms part of your e-mail address. Have alternatives ready since your first choice may be taken by someone else.

4 Make sure the username and password are memorable or write them somewhere safe in case you forget them.

5 If the installation was successful, you will probably be asked to restart your computer and the ISP's icon will show on the Desktop and possibly on the task bar and Start menu as well.

UNIVERSAL E-MAIL

If your Internet connection is provided by a telephone or cable company, then you can only use the e-mail from your own telephone line. The same applies if you are on a network.

If you need to be entirely flexible so as to be able to e-mail from anywhere, then you need to consider signing up with *Hotmail* or *Yahoo* or *ePALS*, who offer web-based e-mail. There are a host of companies offering this flexible connection. Which you choose depends entirely on whom you ask for advice. As teachers, you should strongly consider a filtered and monitored service like that offered by *ePALS.com*.

HINTS AND TIPS

- Before you start, make a note of the helpline number.

- Sometimes the e-mail 'username' and password can be found on the CD cover.

- Instead of the username, you may be asked to insert a registration number – probably from the CD cover.

- If you don't close down all the programs currently running, you may run into 'conflict' problems where something in a program doesn't agree with what you are trying to install.

- You can't use commas, spaces, back and forward slashes or brackets in a username.

- You can use hyphens, underscore and full stops.

- Think of a password at least 5 or 6 letters long and have an 8-letter alternative ready too.

Starting up on a stand-alone PC

When you switch on any computer – laptop or stand-alone – the screen will eventually settle down to something like the one shown below. The screen illustrated below is called the 'desktop' and what appears on it will depend on how the operating system has been set up. In this example the operating system is *Windows*.

DESKTOP

These small pictures are *active* icons – they are clickable short-cuts, which start applications or open files or folders.

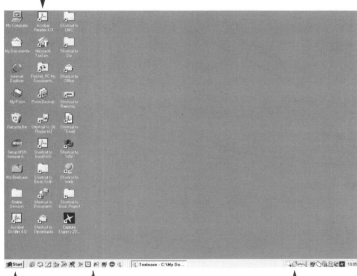

The desktop can have a different background – colour, picture or animation. These features can be accessed and changed by opening the *Properties* with a right-click.

This is the *Start* button.

This is the *Task* bar – it also has short-cuts and shows applications currently running.

This is the *System tray*.

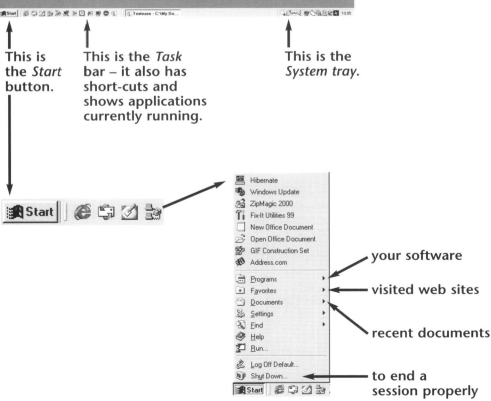

your software

visited web sites

recent documents

to end a session properly

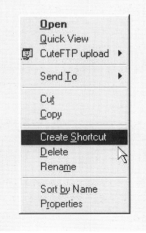

1 These are three very important shortcuts on your desktop.

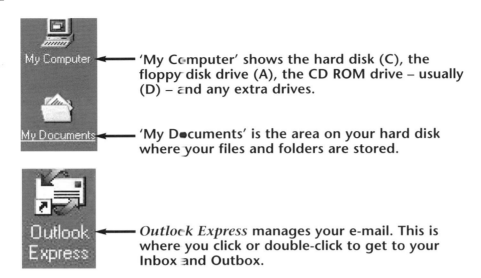

'**My Computer**' shows the hard disk (C), the floppy disk drive (A), the CD ROM drive – usually (D) – and any extra drives.

'**My Documents**' is the area on your hard disk where your files and folders are stored.

Outlook Express manages your e-mail. This is where you click or double-click to get to your **Inbox** and **Outbox.**

Mouse Clicks

Command	Action
'select'	Click on an object with the left mouse button.
'double-click'	Move the pointer over the chosen object and with the left mouse button click twice in quick succession.
'right-click'	Click on an object with the right mouse button to view 'options'/ 'properties' – also to rename or delete.
'drag'	Move the pointer over the object to be dragged, hold down the left mouse button and move the object to its new location before releasing the button.

2 On a PC all data is displayed in windows like the one shown here. Each window has the same features.

maximize button

close button

minimize button

title bar

menu bars

status bar

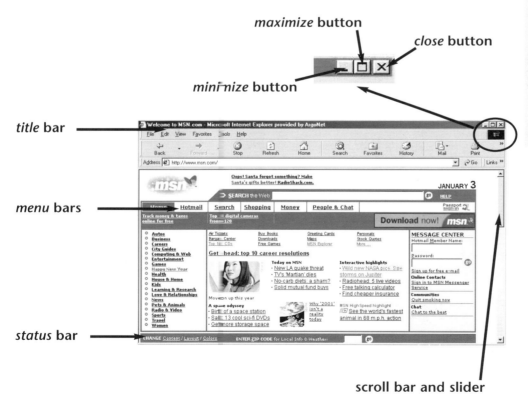

scroll bar and slider

3 Always use the *Shut Down* option to close a session or restart.

Starting up on a network PC

If your school has a network, every computer on it is connected to a central computer called a server. The server stores all the software and operating system and sends copies to all the networked machines.

HINTS AND TIPS

Type in your username and password carefully. You will have to start again if you misspell them, if you put in an extra space, or even if you use a capital letter where it should be lower case.

1 Once you have logged on to a network with your 'username' and password, a screen like this will appear.

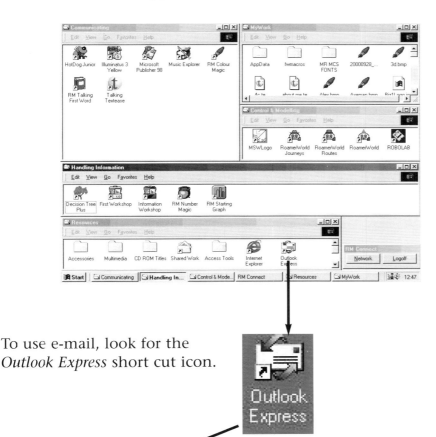

2 To use e-mail, look for the *Outlook Express* short cut icon.

3 Clicking on the icon brings up the starter page of the software.

27

Starting up on an Apple Mac

Most primary schools use *Windows* PCs, so in this book we have focused on using these computers. If your school uses Apple Macintosh computers, the desktop and the opening screens for *Outlook Express* will look different to those on a PC, but the step-by-step techniques for using e-mail are identical.

1 When you switch on an Apple Macintosh computer, the screen will settle down to look something like the one opposite. Double-click the mouse on the Macintosh Hard Drive icon to open the list of folders on your machine. *Outlook Express* is usually contained within the folder marked *Internet*.

2 Double-click on this folder to open your e-mail software.

The *Apple* Icon is located here but a different icon may appear here temporarily depending on the software you are running

This is the *Hard Drive* icon

The Macintosh *Desktop*

The *Wastebasket*: the Macintosh Recycle Bin

Outlook Express **Main Page**

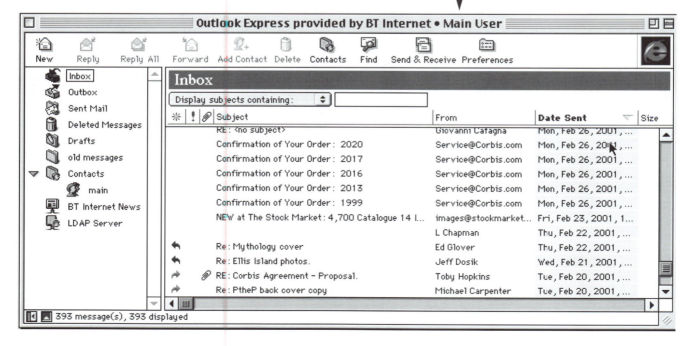

Starting 'Outlook Express'

Outlook Express manages your e-mail activities so you can compose, send and receive e-mails. It enables you to store contact details, including e-mail addresses, in a special electronic address book and attach image and text files for transmission with your messages. You can open *Outlook Express* in one of three ways:

1 From the Desktop . . .

Find the short-cut icon on the desktop and double-click

2 From the Start menu . . .

Click the *Start* button and move the mouse pointer through *Programs* and locate *Outlook Express* on the sub-menu. Click to return.

3 From *Internet Explorer* . . .

Click on the *Mail* button and highlight an option.

4

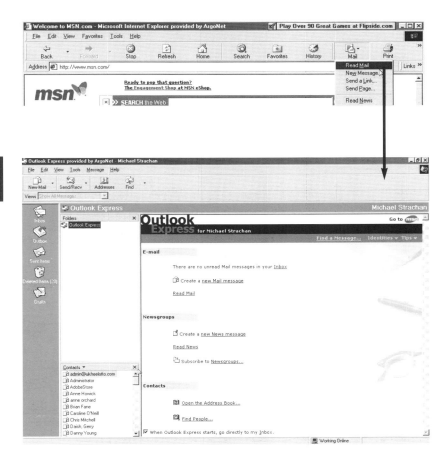

'Outlook Express' main window and panels

Once you have opened the program, you will see a window like the one shown below. Make yourself familiar with the various parts of the window and what each option does.

The *folders* panel contains every folder you create to store your e-mails efficiently.

The *Menu* bar contains all the usual options such as *File* and *Edit* plus *Messages*.

The *Toolbar* lets you access the main features quickly.

The *Outlook bar* has short cuts to the most important folders.

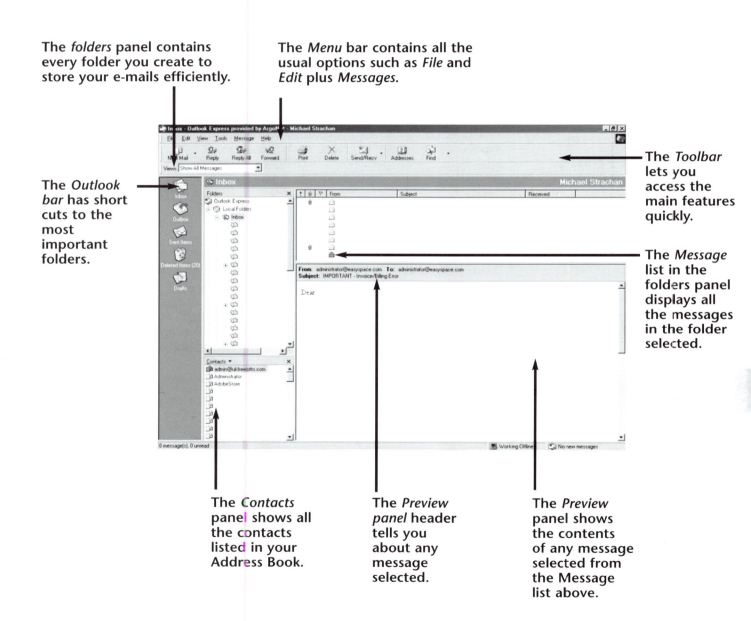

The *Message* list in the folders panel displays all the messages in the folder selected.

The *Contacts* panel shows all the contacts listed in your Address Book.

The *Preview panel* header tells you about any message selected.

The *Preview* panel shows the contents of any message selected from the Message list above.

'Outlook Express' toolbar

Study the toolbar at the top of the window.

New Mail
Opens a blank
e-mail writing
window.

Reply All
Sends reply to
all recipients of
the message.

Print
Click to print
a copy of the
selected e-mail.

Send/Recv
Sends
messages in
the Outbox
and checks for
incoming mail.

Find
To search for
e-mails by
sender and
receiver.

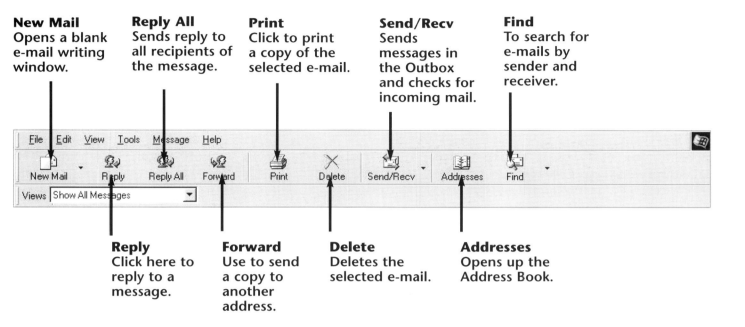

Reply
Click here to
reply to a
message.

Forward
Use to send
a copy to
another
address.

Delete
Deletes the
selected e-mail.

Addresses
Opens up the
Address Book.

If you wish, you can the change the layout of the window and toolbar as follows:

1 From *View* highlight *Layout* and click.

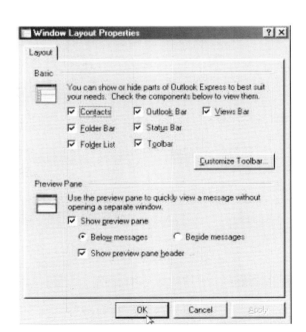

2 Click the options you want and confirm with *OK*.

31

Receiving E-mails . . .

When you go online and start *Outlook Express,* the first thing it does is to check whether you have received any e-mail. Your new messages will be downloaded to your 'Inbox' and you can read them. If you need to, you can do this manually by any of the three methods shown below.

1 From the Toolbar . . .

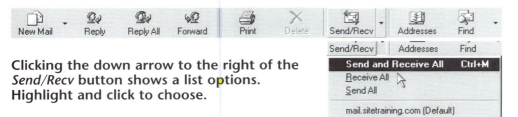

Clicking the down arrow to the right of the *Send/Recv* **button shows a list options. Highlight and click to choose.**

2 From the Menu . . .

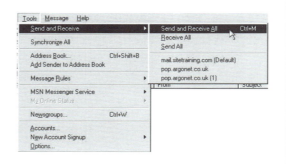

Clicking the *Tools* **button brings up this sub-menu.**

Choose one of the three options by highlighting and clicking .

3 Using the Send/Recv button . . .

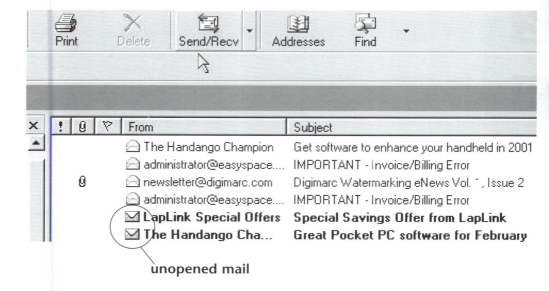

Clicking the *Send/Recv* **button brings up the Message list.**

unopened mail

HINTS AND TIPS

You need to be online to pick up your mail. If you try to do this offline, you will be asked to connect to your Internet Service Provider.

If you don't have any mail waiting to be collected, you will receive a message.

Be patient as you highlight an option because, if it has a further sub-option, this will appear automatically.

TECHNICAL NOTES

If you choose the option to 'Send and Receive All', *Outlook Express* will send any messages waiting in your Outbox at the same time that it checks and receives incoming mail.

The short-cut for 'Send and Receive All' mail is

CTRL + M

. . . and Reading E-mails

Most of the time you will not have to bother with manually displaying your e-mails because *Outlook Express* automatically places and displays your incoming mail in the Inbox. Your new messages are displayed in a Message list like the one shown below. This tells you who sent the messages, the subject of each e-mail and the time it was received.

1 To display the full e-mail, click on the listing in the Message list and the full e-mail will appear in the Preview panel, as you can see in the example below.

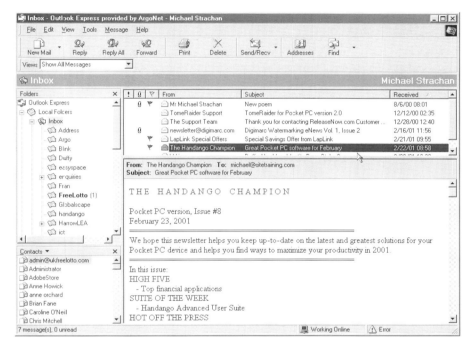

2 If the e-mail is too big for the window, simply scroll up or down to view the entire contents.

3 New and unread messages are displayed in **bold** typeface. Once you have displayed and read them in the Preview panel, the listing changes back to a regular typeface.

To print a message

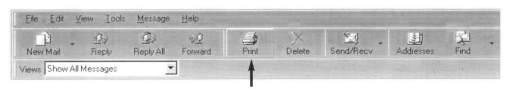

Click the *Print* button and follow the instructions for your printer.

HINTS AND TIPS

When you receive new mail this icon will show on the Task bar.

You can't open the mail from there – you have to do that from your Inbox.

To view an e-mail in a separate new window, move the pointer over it and double-click OR click once over it and press the ENTER key.

You can scroll through the contents of the Message list by using the Up and Down cursor keys.

The short-cut for 'Select all messages' is:

CTRL + A

This short-cut works with many applications.

If you find yourself lost in a maze of e-mails and want to go back to your Inbox, use the shortcut:

CTRL + I

TECHNICAL NOTES

The usual options on printers are:

● print whole document

● print selected text

● print current page

● print from page x to y.

Writing a new message

1 Click the *New Mail* button to bring up this blank *Message* window.

2 Your e-mail address is automatically placed here in the *From* field.

3 Write the e-mail address of the recipient here.

5 Summarise the purpose of the e-mail here.

4 If you need to send 'carbon copies' to other people, put their addresses here.

6 Type the text of your e-mail here.

POINTS FOR PUPILS TO LEARN

1 The most common reason for e-mail going astray or being delayed and returned is that the address has been typed wrongly.

2 Carbon Copying is just a way of sending a copy of a message to another person. It is irritating to receive a copy of a message that is of interest or importance only to one person, so do not overuse the function.

3 Think carefully about the purpose of the e-mail and put a brief summary in the Subject window. If you do not, you will receive a reminder about doing this.

4 If your e-mail is long-winded, no one will read it properly. Only use 'emoticons' and fancy short-cut phrases if you are sure the receiver will quickly understand them. Always sign e-mail as a courtesy gesture, even though your e-mail address will have been recorded.

HINTS AND TIPS

Composing your message offline will save money. When you've finished, save the message and it will be placed automatically in the 'Outbox'. The next time you go online the message will be sent automatically.

Emoticons (keyboard characters arranged to make 'emotional icons' such as a smiling face) can make you

: –) or : – (

Children are sure to enjoy using them. We've included some of them on one of the photocopiable activities along with some short-cut phrases.

Addresses and Writing Style

Getting the address right is just as important when sending e-mail as it is when sending ordinary post.

'User Name' which identifies the person to whom you are sending the e-mail.

The 'Domain' name may be provided by the school or could be from the web site hosted for the school.

The 'country code' is used by all countries except the USA, which does not have one.

sarah@anyprimary.sch.uk ISP E-MAIL ADDRESS

The 'Separator' or 'at' sign looks like a desert rat with a long tail. It separates the User and Domain names.

The suffix can tell you the kind of institution using this address. In the above example, it is a school; in the lower example, it is a web-mail company.

sarah.jones@yahoo.com WEB-MAIL ADDRESS

The User Name should be one that can be remembered easily, although sometimes you cannot get your first choice of user name.

The Domain name may be provided by a company as part of a service you can access anywhere on any computer.

Netiquette (or good E-mail Manners)

- Check your spelling.
- Avoid using all capital letters.
- Keep attachments small.
- Keep your messages short and focused.
- Avoid nasty e-mails at all costs.
- Don't write anything you wouldn't say in public.
- Don't use CC (Carbon Copy) to copy your message to everyone.
- Always include your name at the bottom of the message.
- Avoid sending e-mails to large numbers of people unless you have a reason to do so.
- Clearly summarise the message contents in the subject line.
- Use BCC (Blind Carbon Copy) to copy your message to a large group who don't know each other.

TECHNICAL TIP

A two- or three-letter code in a Web site address indicates the type of organisation the Web site belongs to. A two-letter code such as '.fr' for France or '.jp' for Japan is sometimes used at the end of the address.

Organisation code	Type of organisation
.com	company
.co.uk	UK company
.net	network
.gov	government department
.edu	educational institute
.org	organisation
.org.uk	UK organisation
.ac	university
.sch	school

Setting up an Address Book

The Address Book is really useful for storing the names, details and addresses of people you contact regularly. Once someone is in your address book, you can quickly insert their address into a message or you can make up a group of contacts and send the message to all of them.

You can directly add details to an Address Book either from the Inbox:

1 Right-click on a message from the person you want to include in your Address Book.

2 Highlight the option to *Add Sender to Address Book*. Click.

OR from an opened message:

1 Make sure the message has been opened and is showing in the message panel.

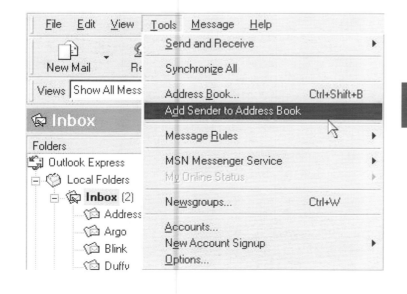

2 Click *Tools*. Highlight the option to *Add Sender to Address Book* and click.

HINTS AND TIPS

Many software packages betray their business origins. *Outlook Express* is no exception, and anyone you write messages to or receive messages from is called a 'contact'.

It saves time and frustration if, when you open up a message you have received, you decide then and there whether this is a contact worth keeping up.

You can put a new contact in your Address Book manually, and automatically, as shown on page 37.

If you are working on a network, every child can have an Address Book which is theirs to update and maintain. Encourage children to edit their address books regularly, deleting old addresses and creating address groups where necessary.

Adding new addresses manually . . .

1 On the Contacts panel, Click *Contacts*, highlight *New Contact* from the drop-down menu and click again.

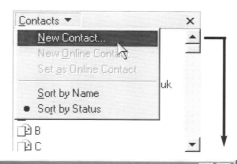

2 Insert the first and last names and the e-mail address of your new contact.

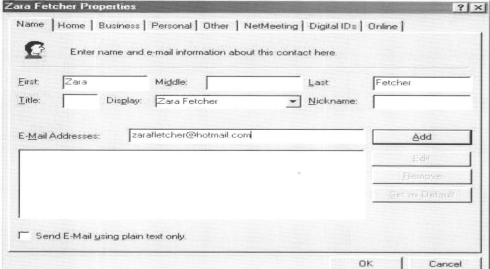

3 Click *Add* to confirm contact.

. . . and automatically

1 Click the Tools menu then highlight and click *Options*.

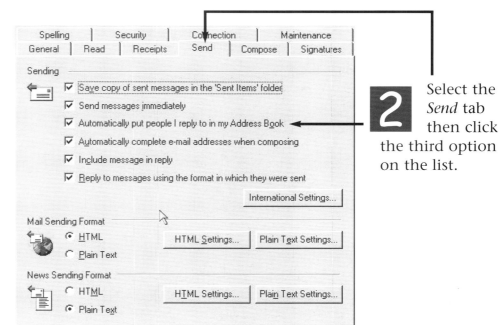

2 Select the *Send* tab then click the third option on the list.

Creating Address Groups

HINTS AND TIPS

Some groups you may want to create are: Your class, Your year group, Your colleagues. Other schools, LEA contacts, Friends and family.

If you need to send e-mails to a group of people regularly, it is helpful to put those contacts together into a 'Group'. *Outlook Express* treats the group as if it were a single contact.

1 Click *Addresses* to open up your Address Book.

2 Click the *New* button and choose *New Group*.

3 Click in the *Group Name* box, and type an appropriate name for your new group.

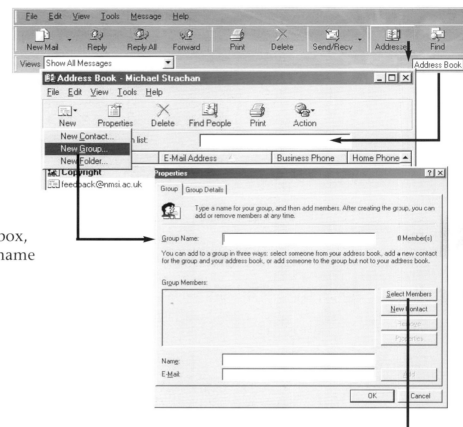

Adding contacts to a Group

1 Click the *Select Members* button shown above and choose *New Contact*.

2 Click on a Contact to highlight and select it by clicking the *Select* button.

3 The new group member will appear in the *Members* box.

4 Continue adding new members in this way and, when you have finished, confirm your choices by clicking the *OK* button.

This is where your new members appear

Individual contact

Replying to messages

You may want to reply directly to an e-mail, or to forward that e-mail to someone else with a comment about its contents. To start this process make sure the message is open.

1 Click on the *Reply* button.

2 The original message is displayed in a new window together with the sender's reply address filled in.

3 Click here and type your own comments/ message before clicking on the send button.

4 If the message was sent to a number of people and you want to reply to all of them, click on the *Reply All* button.

 Click and type your comments/ message as shown above, before sending in the usual way.

Forwarding and carbon copying

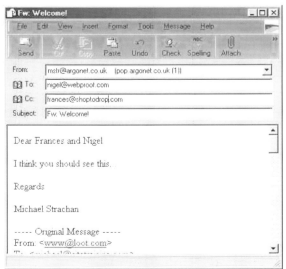

6 Make sure the message is open and click on the *Forward* button.

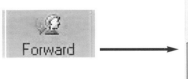

Either type in an address or use one from your address book.

If you click on the *Cc* button your address book will be opened for you to choose an address.

Managing your e-mail 1

As you become more confident in sending and receiving e-mails, you will need to think about organising and managing them in folders and sub-folders.

To create a new folder

1 Click on any folder icon – for example the *Inbox* . . .

. . . and right-click to bring up this menu.

2 Choose *New Folder* and click to show the *Create Folder* window.

3 Type in a suitable name for your new folder . . .

4 . . . and confirm by clicking *OK*.

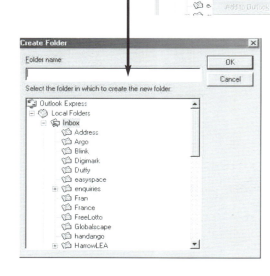

HINTS AND TIPS

Once the e-mails start flowing in, you will need to set up folders in which to store them, otherwise you will lose track of them.

You may want folders for mail from:

● your headteacher
● from other classes
● from other schools
● from newsgroup members
● from the LEA
● from family and friends

To create sub-folders

1 Open up the *Create Folder* window and highlight click on the folder in which you are going to create a sub-folder.

2 Click the right mouse button and choose *New folder*. Insert the appropriate name for the new folder and confirm by clicking *OK*.

Any main folder containing other folders shows a plus sign.

Clicking on the plus sign opens up the sub-folder.

Clicking on the 'minus' sign closes the sub-folder.

40

Managing your e-mail 2

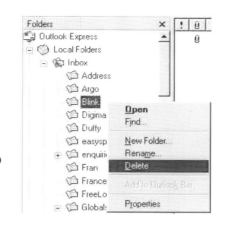

Deleting a folder

1 Click on any folder icon . . .

. . . and right-click to bring up this menu.

2 Click the *Delete* option and confirm.

Moving messages

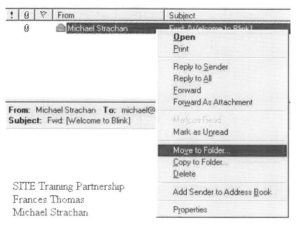

1 Click on an e-mail message . . .

. . . and right-click to bring up this menu.

2 Click the *Move to Folder* option.

3 Click on another folder to highlight and confirm your choice for the move by clicking *OK*.

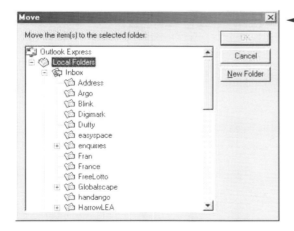

4 If you need to make a *New Folder* click that button and follow the instructions.

Saving your e-mail

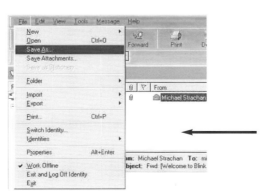

1 Click on *File* and choose *Save As* . . . from the menu.

2 Follow the on-screen instructions to save to the area of your choice.

Attachments

Attachments are files that are transmitted along with your e-mail. They can be images, word-processed files, video clips, *Adobe Acrobat* files or forms, and so on.

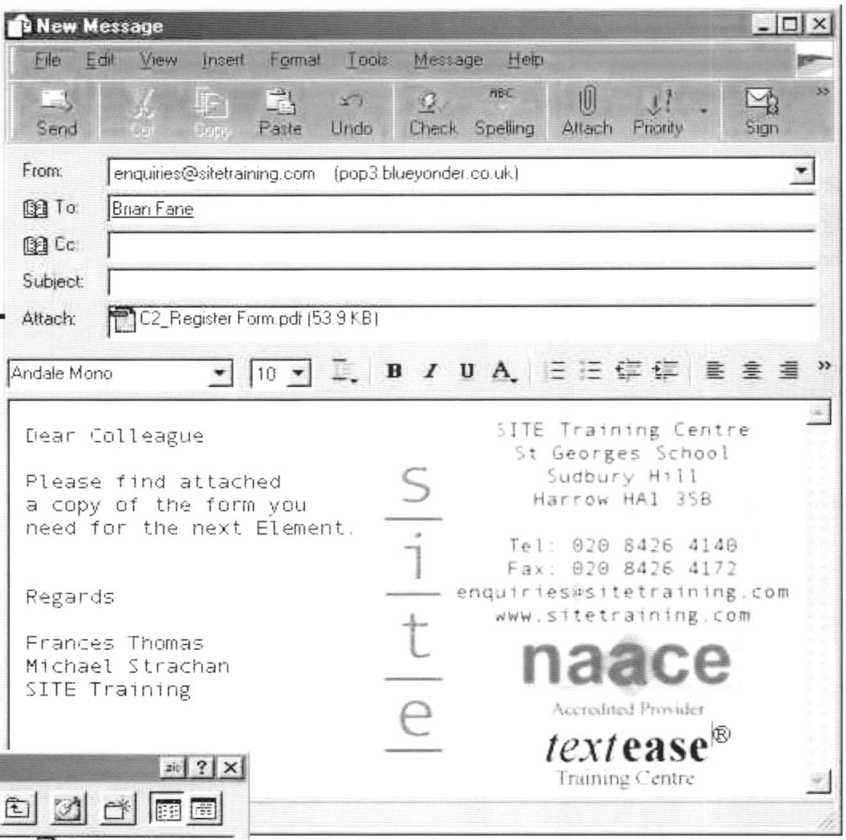

1 To attach a file, first ensure that a message window is open like the one shown here. Insert the address and the subject line.

2 Click on the *Attach* button to open up the *Insert Attachment* window.

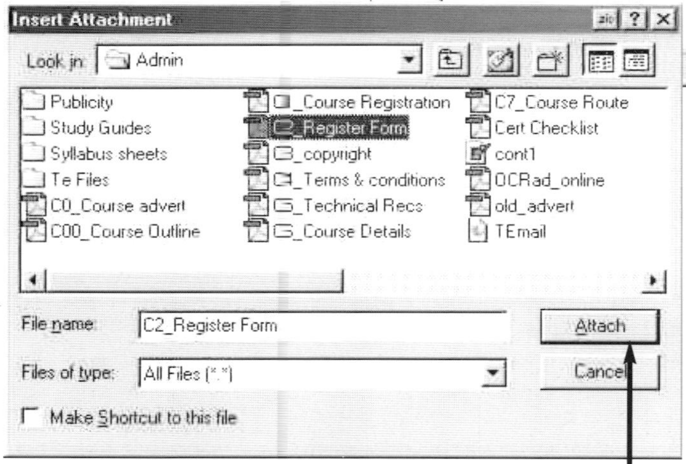

3 Click on the file to insert it in the *File name* box.

4 Click on the *Attach* button to complete the attachment process.

5 Click to send the e-mail in the usual way.

HINTS AND TIPS

Typical attachments might be: for a History project, a picture of Henry VIII; for a Geography project, a photograph of a volcano; and for an Art project, a copy of a painting from an encyclopedia web site. Remember to check on the copyright situation before you start.

How to handle attachments

Attachments are often huge and can be dangerous. Large attachments will take many minutes to download. Attachments may include viruses. Be wary about downloading anything you were not expecting.

To download an attached file

1 When a message arrives with an attachment, display the full e-mail by clicking on the listing in the Message list. The full e-mail will appear in the Preview panel like the one shown here.

2 Double-click on the paper-clip icon to show the attached file as shown above.

3 Click *Save Attachments* to open access to your filing system. Save in the usual way to a folder of your choice.

IF YOU HAVE ANY DOUBTS ABOUT the origin and purpose of the e-mail and its attachment, do not hesitate to right-click on the listing in the Message panel and use the delete option.

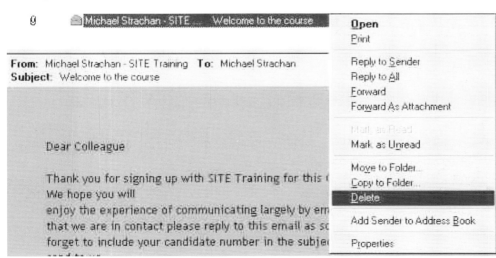

4 This will remove the message and the suspect attachment.

Newsgroups and Chatrooms

Finding new friends who share common interests on the Internet can be a rich experience for children, leading to the sharing of ideas and understanding of other peoples, places and cultures. Newsgroups, discussion boards and 'chatrooms' offer online areas where such interaction can take place. All involve typing in information for others to read – hence the possible danger of becoming involved with unsuitable contacts.

There are various organisations that specialise in providing safe areas where children can meet each other on the Internet. One of these is *ePals*. Its web site address is given in Section 5. The site offers teacher-designed interactive projects, monitored e-mail, instant translation, discussion boards, private chat, maps, e-cards, international weather and more.

Using a secure system such as *ePals* to collaborate and communicate takes the anxieties out of using e-mail, discussion boards and live chat areas.

To use 'Outlook Express' for online notices, debate and discussion

As a teacher, you may want to share your experiences in the classroom with others. As a parent of a pupil, you may want to exchange ideas with other parents about events in your school. Newgroups provide the ideal way for you to communicate.

1 Click the *Tools* button and look for *Newsgroups*.

2 After several minutes of downloading thousands of potentially interesting groups, you will see something like this screen.

3 Put in a word to describe the kind of newsgroup you are interested in and click *Go to* to sample the selection.

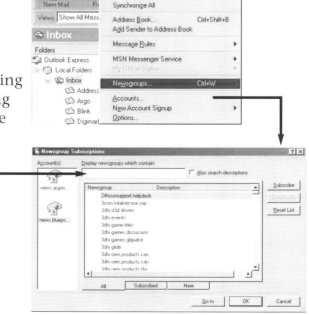

SECTION 3:
QUESTIONS AND ANSWERS

Q What Can I Do When The Equipment Fails?   46

Q What Can I Do About Software Problems And Viruses?   46

Q How Can I Avoid Losing an E-mail Connection?   46

Q What Is An Attachment?   47

Q How Can I Speed Up My E-mail?   47

Q Why Am I Experiencing Address Problems?   47

Q Why Have I Been Disconnected?   48

Q What Type Of Hardware Problems Can I Fix And How?   48

Q Where Can I Find Help When I Need It?   48

Q Where Can I Find Help When I Am At Home?   49

Q How Secure Is E-mail?   49

Q How Can I Make The Most Of Limited Resources?   50

Q Can I Use My E-mail Address Anywhere In The World?   50

Q How Do I Know Whether My E-mail Has Been Sent?   50

Q Why Has My E-mail Been Returned?   51

Q Why Does It Sometimes Take So Long For My Message To Arrive?   51

Q What Should I Do If I Do Not Recognise An E-mail?   51

Q WHAT CAN I DO WHEN THE EQUIPMENT FAILS?

A Computers sometimes 'freeze' or 'crash'. The more up-to-date your operating system, the less likely this is to happen. Holding down the CONTROL and ALT keys and pressing the DELETE key will usually identify the fault and the system may provide advice on what to do next.

If nothing appears to work, consult your manual about using the re-set button. This is a small button, usually concealed in a recess, that closes down and restarts your computer. When it starts up, you will almost certainly see a blue warning screen with a message about checking your hard disk for error. Don't panic – the message usually clears without any further problem.

If you are using a network and everything seizes up, make the ICT co-ordinator or network manager aware but don't restart or switch off the computer. Leave it so the manager can read any warning message that has appeared on screen.

Q WHAT CAN I DO ABOUT SOFTWARE PROBLEMS AND VIRUSES?

A Many unexpected software problems that produce strange 'error messages' on screen can be sorted out by closing down your machine and restarting it. If possible, log off the e-mail phone connection or shut down your machine in the proper way.

Viruses can find their way into your hard drive and corrupt your software or operating software. One precaution is to avoid, or restrict the use of, floppy disks. Another is not to open any e-mails from sources you do not recognise or with suspicious subject titles. Many schools now do this. Ensure your system is equipped with an up-to-date virus checker for examing disks and files. You can download latest versions of anti-virus software from the Internet.

Q HOW CAN I AVOID LOSING AN E-MAIL CONNECTION?

A E-mail programs such as *Outlook Express* are complex pieces of software and are prone to unexpected glitches. Save messages as 'drafts' as you go along. Sometimes a lost connection can be sorted out by pressing the REFRESH button at the top of the screen page.

Q WHAT IS AN ATTACHMENT?

A An attachment is something that has been added to an e-mail. It may be a document, a file or a picture.

If the attached file is very large, the e-mail will take a long time to be sent or received. If you can, it is a good idea to compress a large file using 'Winzip' or 'ZipMagic', although the receiver will need a copy of this software to decompress the file.

If you receive an attachment, you will have to click on it and open it separately in order to see the contents. You can then save the file in any folder.

Q HOW CAN I SPEED UP MY E-MAIL?

A Start by considering why you are experiencing delays. It could just be that there are too many people trying to use your provider's computers and all the lines are engaged.

There seem to be certain times of day when it's difficult to get online and you just have to try later. For example, the time when people in the UK are checking their e-mail and browsing the Internet in the evening, when phone fees are low, corresponds with when people in the United States are waking up and doing the same. If you notice one particular time of day is better than another for sending e-mail, use this period to send large video, image and sound files as they are often made up of huge amounts of data.

Don't forget that you can write your e-mails when you are offline. Write your messages in batches and store them in your outbox to be sent when you next go online.

If you are using e-mail from home on old equipment, it may be that your modem is slow. You should be using at least a 56K modem if you want to send large attachments. However, large files – more than 1 Mb – may still take several minutes to be sent.

Q WHY AM I EXPERIENCING ADDRESS PROBLEMS?

A If you are trying to connect to the Internet to send or receive e-mail, check that your user name and password are correct and have been typed in accurately.

47

Check, too, that the address to which you want to send a message has been keyed in correctly. Some e-mail addresses have dashes, underscored lines or full stops in between names.

If you are using web-mail, be sure to type in the correct URL. One small mistake (such as mixing up upper-case and lower-case letters, or using the wrong character) could take you to a dead-end.

Q WHY HAVE I BEEN DISCONNECTED?

A If you are using a modem that is used for your telephone or fax machine, you may be disconnected if you try to use one of these pieces of equipment at the same time. Some ISPs operate a time-out on their connection. So if you don't use the computer for a while, the connection is severed.

It often happens that you are disconnected while you are trying to send very large files. E-mail software can be set up to reject incoming e-mails beyond a certain size (usually those with very large attachments) or it may be that the message is taking so long to download that you exceed your ISP's time-out period.

Q WHAT TYPE OF HARDWARE PROBLEMS CAN I FIX AND HOW?

A The good news is that you don't have to be a computer expert to keep things going. Here are a few tips:

● If you switch on your computer at home or in the classroom and nothing happens, first check whether the plugs to the main power supply are secure and switched on.

● If you come back to a computer that has been in use and the screen is blank, it may just be that it is in power-saving mode. Jiggle the mouse and the screen may reappear.

● If a printer stops working, check that the ink cartridges or toner cartridge are not empty and that there is sufficient dry, clean, uncreased paper in the feeder.

If the problem persists, speak to someone more experienced.

Q WHERE CAN I FIND HELP WHEN I NEED IT?

A If you are a classroom teacher, then your first port of call is your ICT network manager, co-ordinator or more experienced colleague. If your LEA has an advisory service, you can approach them for help.

Some LEAs use private agencies and companies for support and training instead. Your advisory teacher would be able to point you in the right direction.However, some schools use an independent advisor. She or he will regularly visit the school and offer practical help with hardware and software. Network managers and ICT co-ordinators should have an ISP hotline or be able to call on the installation company to sort out some problems.

Q WHERE CAN I FIND HELP WHEN I AM AT HOME?

A If you have signed up with an Internet Access Provider or Internet Service Provider that has a free support hotline, try calling the number. Usually someone at the other end will take you through each step of the installation process and supply any missing information.

If you only have one telephone line, this form of support is more difficult as you cannot carry out the instructions simultaneously. Another problem is that the lines are often engaged.

Q HOW SECURE IS E-MAIL?

A In general, any e-mail you send is likely to have a safe and secure passage. However, it is a public system and therefore is not the medium for sending sensitive information.

It is far better to communicate such matters over the telephone or, better still, face-to-face in a quiet setting. During transit, an e-mail passes through your ISP's server and your recipient's server. There is always a small chance that it could be copied en route. However, this caution really only applies to extremely sensitive information.

A more common danger is sending hasty e-mails. The great advantage of e-mail is speed. The disadvantage is that once you have commited your thoughts to e-mail and click to send, there is no way to recall it!

Receiving e-mails regularly poses problems of its own. If you don't recognise where an e-mail has come from or you don't know the sender, be very careful. Apart from the dangers of being sent unpleasant and vicious mail, there is the danger of virus attack.

Increasingly, e-mail attachments are being used to send virus infections. These are designed to infect your address book and will spread to all your friends and contacts. If you are not sure of an attachment, however attractive its disguise, delete it. Remember, an infected attachment can come from a friend, so check it if you have any doubt, by contacting the friend another way.

If you have an Internet policy in place within the school and parents use a filtered system and occasionally monitor what children are using and how often, then you are taking reasonable precautions. In Section 5 of the books, we have provided some links to LEAs and agencies who provide specimen policies that schools can use for their own needs.

Q HOW CAN I MAKE THE MOST OF LIMITED RESOURCES?

A In an ideal world, each child would have access to his or her own computer to use as and when appropriate. However, in the majority of schools, teachers have to timetable computer use with great care.

If there is one computer in a classroom, collaborative work with small groups of children working on directed tasks is the best option. Even where there is a network of computers, this resource still has to be carefully timetabled to provide equal access. These issues need to be discussed together by the whole teaching staff.

At home, you will also be on a limited budget. Consider carefully the issues of upgrading hardware and software. It is not necessary to upgrade to a later version of a program each time one comes out. Make sure you buy to suit your own needs.

Q CAN I USE MY E-MAIL ADDRESS ANYWHERE 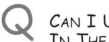 IN THE WORLD?

A To use any e-mail, you must have an ISP connection – someone to provide you with a connection.

If you have web-based mail, such as *yahoo.com, hotmail.com* or *ePALS.com*, then you can send and receive mail from any other location. If you have been given an e-mail address in school or at home, then you can only pick up or send mail from there.

Q HOW DO I KNOW WHETHER MY E-MAIL HAS BEEN SENT?

A Check your 'Sent' mail box. It will tell you whether you have any unsent messages. Look for a folder 'Sent items' and double-click to open it. You should see a list of any recent messages you have sent.

Q WHY HAS MY E-MAIL BEEN RETURNED?

A There are occasions when e-mails cannot be delivered and are returned to you. They may be marked 'Message Undeliverable: User Unknown', which means that the address should be checked and may not have been exact.

Sometimes messages come back because there is a problem with the server and routers on the Internet. Often, messages that 'bounce back' are re-sent automatically a few hours later, but after two or three failed attempts, the system gives up.

Q WHY DOES IT SOMETIMES TAKE SO LONG FOR MY MESSAGE TO ARRIVE?

A If there is a technical problem with the server used by the sender or recipient, the messages may take days to arrive. Some ISPs only send or receive messages at regular intervals.

Q WHAT SHOULD I DO IF I DO NOT RECOGNISE AN E-MAIL?

A Be very careful. Sometimes viruses can be transferred via an e-mail message with an attachment. If in doubt, do not open the message and especially do not open the attachment. Delete it if you can or call the network manager or ICT co-ordinator.

SECTION 4: Photocopiable Projects

1	Getting in touch	56
2	Weigh it up	57
3	Drafting a message	58
4	Mystery messages	59
5	Making e-friends	60
6	Dot what?	61
7	E-news report	62
8	Make a joke chain	63
9	Make up a story	64
10	Story cards	65
11	A list poem	66
12	Leisure time	67
13	My journey to school	68
14	Holiday survey	69
15	A legend	70
16	An invitation	71
17	Career interview	72
18	Healthy eating	73
19	Comparing costs	74
20	Animal habitats: 1	75
21	Animal habitats: 2	76
22	Maths tips	77
23	Recycling questionnaire	78
24	Ask an expert: 1	79
25	Ask an expert: 2	80
26	A local walk	81
27	A local hero	82
28	Music review	83
29	Life in another country	84
30	Abbreviations	85
31	Smileys	86
32	Signing off	87

Teachers' notes

The following photocopiable activities are designed to help children improve their ICT and writing skills. The projects link with literacy work by encouraging children to consider the purpose and audience of e-mails, learn how to draft and edit messages, and appreciate how e-mail can be used to gather and share information in all kinds of areas. The activity sheets are also valuable assessment tools.

Most of the projects can be completed by children working in groups. The activities generally contain an off-screen element where the children work on paper, followed by an on-screen activity. It is a good idea for children to compose all e-mails offline and go online only to send and receive mail.

It is not expected that the activities will be completed in one lesson, and at the end of each sheet there is a suggestion for a **Next step**, or a way of extending the project. Several of the suggestions involve planning for a group project, such as creating a display, which may be completed over a number of lessons.

Many projects ask the children to exchange e-mails with pupils at other schools. This is an ideal way for them to compare experiences and learn about different locations. The teacher will need to set up links with other schools in advance of the project, which can be done through 'ePALS.com Classroom Exchange' (see Section 5).

Through ePALS, teachers can set up secure accounts for children which they can monitor and control. Every effort is made to ensure the privacy and safety of children and teachers. It is essential that teachers use or recommend only web sites and organisations that guarantee a filtered, monitored and secure e-mail service. The following notes provide suggestions for ways of making the most of the activities and introducing, adapting or extending them.

Getting in touch (page 56)
The children may need ideas to get them started, for example, telephone, e-mail, fax, written letter, mobile phone text message, whistle, flare. For the Next step, the children will need access to books, CD-ROMs and web sites that feature the history of communication. You could mask and substitute some of the pictures to make the historical element relevant to the period the children are studying.

Weigh it up (page 57)
With the whole class, discuss the children's ideas. You could suggest extra things they may not have thought of, for example, how secure/confidential the information is, how e-mail can be a better way of communicating with people in countries with different time-zones. Regarding the cost, you could explain that to send an e-mail anywhere in the world, you pay only for the time you spend online, at local call rates. Fax transmissions are charged at standard telephone call rates. For the Next step, you could set up a class-to-class partnership with another local school. You could also discuss how the different systems have been improved).

Drafting a message (page 58)
You can use this activity to introduce children to drafting, writing and editing e-mails. Emphasise that they should compose e-mails carefully and check their spelling before sending it.

Mystery messages (page 59)
This activity prompts children to think about writing e-mails for different purposes. They should appreciate that an unsolicited e-mail to someone not known personally should provide a clear explanation and should not contain slang. Discuss e-mail conventions, such as opening and closing remarks.

Making e-friends (page 60)
Help the children to find e-mail addresses of other children with whom they can build a friendship via e-mail. You could set up links with another school, or use ePALS.com Classroom Exchange (see Section 5). This activity can help the children to make first contact. They could think of things they would like to know about the other person and write questions in the e-mail.

Dot what? (page 61)
This activity can be completed in preparation for corresponding with pupils in a foreign country, as part of a school-to-school project. It can also be used as a starting point for a database activity, with database fields for nationality and the different parts of an e-mail address. Introduce the project by explaining that e-mails can be sent to people all over the world. Country codes help to identify the location of a company or organisation. Although there is no obligation for a company to include the country code in their e-mail address, many do so. Provide newspapers, magazines and leaflets from a variety of sources (for example, publications by schools, charities and international organisations) that contain e-mail addresses.

E-news report (page 62)
You could introduce this activity by discussing with the whole class the different tasks that need to be done when producing a newspaper or informative leaflet, such as gathering news and quotes, copy-editing, preparing the circulation list and so on. The project could be done in a group, with different people assigned to different tasks. The children could scan in a photograph to include with the report. If so, they should keep the file size of the attachment small.

Make a joke chain (page 63)

It will be helpful if the children have already set up e-mail friendships with children in other English-speaking countries. Discuss differences in language between English-speaking countries and the need to explain some jokes to their e-friends.

Make up a story (page 64)

E-mail is ideal for exchanging and editing work speedily. Before the children start writing their stories, you could ask them to decide how many paragraphs there will be in total and roughly how long each should be. Give them a copy of the Story cards sheet on page 65. They could e-mail their finished draft to another pair of children or to children at another school and ask them to comment and suggest improvements.

Story cards (page 65)

Use this page with Make up a story on page 64. Ask the children to cut out the cards. They take turns to pick a card and try to include the idea in their paragraph. They need not use the idea if they don't find it helpful. As an alternative activity, a story could be passed around the whole class, with each child writing a paragraph. Give each child a story card with an idea for them to include.

A list poem (page 66)

The children should jot down ideas on the sheet and then choose the best ones to include in their verse. Encourage them to consider the rhythm of the poem and potential for alliteration when they write the verse. The final illustrated poems would be ideal for a classroom display.

Leisure time (page 67)

Discuss with the children how to group leisure activities into categories, for example, grouping swimming and playing football into the category 'playing sport'. If desired, the activities can be masked and others inserted that the children have chosen for themselves. They could also draw up the table in a word-processing program.

My journey to school (page 68)

Arrange for the children to send their e-mails to pupils at a school in a contrasting location (for example, if your school is in a city and children come to school by bus or train, set up a link with a school in a village where children might walk to school). Pupils at the other school should undertake the same exercise. As a further extension, the children could do a survey of how far pupils travel to school. They could produce graphs to show the results and compare the two schools.

Holiday survey (page 69)

After filling in the information on the suitcase, the children could go on to write a postcard to a friend from their holiday destination.

A legend (page 70)

Use this activity in conjunction with literacy work on myths and legends. You could adapt the sheet to focus on legends the class has studied. The children will need books, CD-ROMs and web site addresses where they can find the legends featured. This project could be a collaboration between two classes in different schools, with the legends to be researched decided on beforehand. The research could be done simultaneously, so that the exchange of e-mails takes place on the same day. The children could reply to the e-mails with questions or requests for more information.

An invitation (page 71)

Provide the children with details of a forthcoming event in the school and e-mail addresses of people to whom they can send the invitation. If the children send the attachments they create in the Next step, they should be aware that the recipient may not have compatible software for opening the attachment. They should also send the information contained in the attachment as e-mail body text.

Career interview (page 72)

For this activity, you will first need to approach people who work in the local community and ask if they are willing to take part in e-mail interviews. Try to obtain the e-mail addresses of a range of people to give the children as wide a choice as possible, and remind the interviewees to give age-appropriate responses. Introduce the activity by showing the children books that explain different jobs and asking them to make notes about what various jobs involve. Pupils who interview people in the same job can share their information and write their reports together.

Healthy eating (page 73)

Introduce the topic by discussing with the whole class why it is important to eat healthily. Explain which foods are essential for a balanced diet (such as energy foods and fruit and vegetables) and which foods they should try not to eat too much of (such as foods high in fat or sugar). You could provide leaflets, books and CD-ROMs containing further information to help them complete the activity.

Comparing costs (page 74)

For this activity, you will first need to establish a link with a school in another country (ensuring that the participants speak English well enough to be able to understand the questionnaire). You could complete the questions as a whole class, using an approximate average of individual children's answers. Provide newspapers or suitable web site addresses which show currency exchange rates. The children may need help to convert the foreign currency prices into sterling.

Animal habitats: 1 and 2 (page 75 and page 76)
For this project you will need to visit a local habitat with the children to look for animals. Arrange a link with another school which can investigate a different habitat, for example: an inner city school could link up with one in the countryside, or an inland school could link up with one on the coast. The activity enables children to learn about different habitats, compare and contrast them, and consider the benefits and problems of using e-mail to share information. When looking for animals, encourage the children to look under stones, on leaves and so on. (Ensure they wash their hands afterwards.)

Maths tips (page 77)
You could introduce the activity by asking the class what rules they know for recognising odd and even numbers, adding two or three even numbers, recognising multiples of certain numbers, and so on. Encourage them to look for patterns in the final digits or the sums of the digits. The children could swap tips with pupils from a class in another school. The whole class could then share the maths tips they have collected and use them for a display.

Recycling questionnaire (page 78)
Introduce the topic by talking to the children about why it is important to recycle and how it can be done. The children could produce bar charts showing the number of classes that recycle each type of rubbish.

Ask an expert: 1 (page 79)
Provide a range of local newspapers, leaflets, books and magazines. Newspapers and magazines in particular often contain the e-mail addresses of contributors. For the Next step the children will need to have experience of using search engines.

Ask an expert: 2 (page 80)
The children are more likely to receive a useful reply if they write to an address which contains a person's name (rather than ones which begin 'info@'). They could add a few personal details in their e-mails to capture the interest of the recipient. Explain that some people, such as celebrities or professional authors, do not reply to unsolicited e-mails because they receive too many, so the children should not be put off if they do not receive a reply.

A local walk (page 81)
The children could exchange their e-mails with pupils at another local school. They will need access to a selection of local history information sources, such as books, leaflets, CD-ROMs and newspaper articles. They could write directions for the walk based on the route they have drawn on the map. They could also scan in photographs of the buildings and send them as e-mail attachments.

A local hero (page 82)
This activity can be done as an e-mail exchange with another school. You could first discuss with the children the kind of information that could be included in a biography. Provide them with books about the local area, along with old and recent local newspapers. The children could try to find out more about the person by visiting the local library. They could scan in a photograph of the person to accompany the text.

Music review (page 83)
The children will need to be familiar with listening to sound files on the Internet and downloading them. You could introduce the activity by talking about different types of music (such as classical, jazz, pop, rock, folk) and their typical characteristics. E-mails could be exchanged with pupils at another school. Groups of children may wish to put together a top ten tunes, chart or choose a composer/singer of the month to review.

Life in another country (page 84)
For this activity, you will first need to establish a link with a school in another country (ensuring that the participants speak English well enough to be able to understand the questionnaire). The greater the difference in lifestyle and culture between the two countries, the more the children will benefit from the project.

Abbreviations (page 85)
Make sure the children do not use abbreviations that are too complicated or obscure. You could ask them to swap their ideas with a friend and try to work out the meanings. The second part of the activity links with word-level work on homonyms.

Smileys (page 86)
Smileys are a useful way of showing the tone of an e-mail. To introduce the activity, discuss with the children the differences between communicating by e-mail and talking to someone in person or on the telephone (for example, by e-mail you cannot tell the person's tone of voice and so it is harder to tell whether they are joking/upset and so on).

Signing off (page 87)
Ensure that the children do not devise signatures that are very long or complicated, as they may not display properly if the recipient has different e-mail software. You could suggest that the children try signatures that include favourite lines from poems or plays, or amusing sayings, puns or tongue-twisters.

Getting in touch

There are many different ways you can get in touch with someone. For each situation, think of a different way of communicating.

Situation		Way of communicating
Telling your mum you'll be late home from school.		*Make a telephone call*
Getting help if you're stuck in a rainforest!		
Telling a friend you're having a great holiday		
Swapping news with a friend in Australia		
Inviting someone to a party		

With your group, discuss your choices.

Next step

● *These are some of the ways people sent messages before modern ways of communicating were invented.*

smoke signals

mail sent by train   telegraph machines

● *Choose one of these ways of communicating.*
● *Find out more about it. Use books, CD-Roms or web sites.*

Weigh it up

For each way of communicating, write one advantage and one disadvantage.

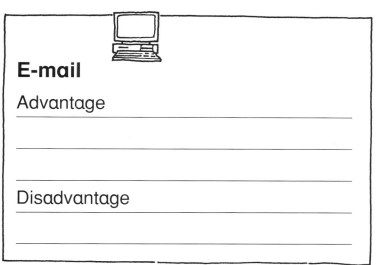

E-mail

Advantage

_____

_____

Disadvantage

_____

_____

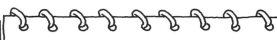

Think about

- how long it takes
- how much it costs
- what equipment you need
- what types of information you can send
- how reliable it is

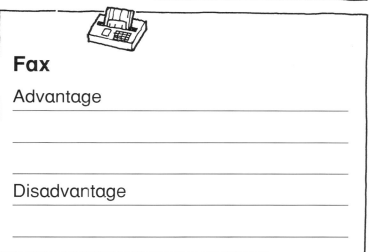

Fax

Advantage

_____

_____

Disadvantage

_____

_____

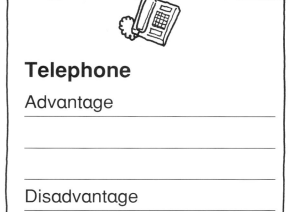

Telephone

Advantage

_____

_____

Disadvantage

_____

_____

Posted letter

Advantage   Disadvantage

_____   _____

_____   _____

_____   _____

Next step
- With your group, send a message by e-mail, posted letter, fax and telephone.
- Make a chart showing how long it takes to receive a reply to each message.

Internet Projects for Primary Schools
Using E-mail
© A & C Black 2001

Drafting a message

Use e-mail to make a collection of book reviews.

First, draft an e-mail asking a friend to tell you about the last book he or she read.

Think about
- how long it takes to write your e-mail
- how you will start your e-mail
- what you will ask
- how you will finish your e-mail

Write your message in the box.

Re-read your message on screen.

How can you improve it? Edit the message.

Write down the changes you make.

Don't forget to write a title in the Subject box.

Check your spelling.

Send the message.

Next step
- When you receive your friend's review, send a reply to thank him or her for helping you with your project.

Internet Projects for Primary Schools
Using E-mail
© A & C Black 2001

Mystery messages

For each e-mail, tick whether you think it is written to a friend or a stranger.

Underline the words and phrases that tell you.

Subject: Request for information
I would like to know what there is to do in Inverness. Please could you send me any details you have. Best wishes Graham Harris

Friend ☐   Stranger ☐

Subject: Plans for Saturday
Hi. Do you know what time the coach leaves on Saturday morning? Thanks

Friend ☐   Stranger ☐

Subject: <untitled>
Have you read Harry Potter and the Goblet of Fire? I thought it was really cool. Zoe

Friend ☐   Stranger ☐

Subject: FAO the librarian
I am a pupil at Park Lane School. I am doing a project on local history. Do you have any information on this subject please? With thanks. Shazia Zia

Friend ☐   Stranger ☐

Subject: Monday evening
My mum said I can't go out on Monday. Sorry. Can you ask someone else instead?

Friend ☐   Stranger ☐

Subject: Missing CD
Dear Sir/Madam Two weeks ago I ordered a CD. Please send it as soon as possible. Thank you.

Friend ☐   Stranger ☐

Next step
- *Write three <u>differences</u> you notice between the e-mails to strangers and friends.*
- *Write reasons why e-mails to strangers need to be different from e-mails to friends.*

Internet Projects for Primary Schools
Using E-mail
© A & C Black 2001

Making e-friends

Use this page to plan how you will introduce yourself to a new e-mail friend.

| My name | My age |

Where I live

My pets

What I look like

My family

Where I go to school

My hobbies

Other things about me

Subjects I like at school

Subjects I don't like at school

Next step
- Use your notes to help you write an e-mail introducing yourself to a new friend.
- Send the e-mail to your new friend.

Think about the order of the information.

Internet Projects for Primary Schools
Using E-mail
© A & C Black 2001

Dot what?

An e-mail address tells you about where the message comes from.

fredcooper@outdoorsports.co.uk

Person's name — 'At' — Name of organisation — Type of organisation — Country code

Match these e-mail addresses with what you think the ending means.

US e-mail addresses don't have a code.

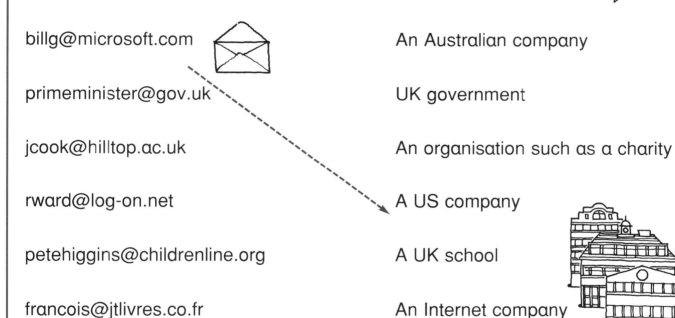

billg@microsoft.com

primeminister@gov.uk

jcook@hilltop.ac.uk

rward@log-on.net

petehiggins@childrenline.org

francois@jtlivres.co.fr

pblake@brilliantgames.co.au

An Australian company

UK government

An organisation such as a charity

A US company

A UK school

An Internet company

A French company

Find some more e-mail addresses.
Write down what they tell you about the person.

Split the address into parts.

Next step
- Go to one of these web sites:
  www.epals.com   www.learningalive.co.uk
- Look at the e-mail addresses of people in the penpal section.
- Write down some more country codes and what they stand for.

Internet Projects for Primary Schools
Using E-mail
© A & C Black 2001

E-news report

You are going to e-mail a news report to teachers at your school. It will be about something your class has done.

> It could be about a sports event or an outing.

Plan your report here.

> Headline

> First paragraph – say what event you are reporting. Say when it happened and who took part.

> Describe what happened. Use sub-headings.

> Write some quotes as direct speech.

> Write a final paragraph to round off the report.

In a word-processing program, write the report. Save it on your hard disk.

> Check your spelling.

Create an e-mail addressed to several teachers at your school.

Attach your news report to the e-mail. Send the e-mail.

Next step
- In your e-mail address book, create a group of the people you sent the report to.
- Edit your report to put on the school web site.

> Think about your audience and style of writing.

Internet Projects for Primary Schools
Using E-mail
© A & C Black 2001

Make a joke chain

Read how to make a joke chain.

Send a joke by e-mail to one of your friends (this is friend I).	Friend I adds a joke and forwards the whole message to friend 2.	Friend 2 adds a joke and forwards the message to Friend 3.
You should get back a message with five different jokes!	Friend 4 adds a joke and forwards the message to you.	Friend 3 adds a joke and forwards the message to Friend 4.

Make your own joke chain. First, find and write the e-mail addresses of four friends.

I. _____   3. _____

2. _____   4. _____

Now find a joke.

Joke _____

_____

_____

You could look in a joke book for ideas.

Use your friends' names instead of 'friend I', 'friend 2' and so on.

Write your e-mail message.
In the message, explain to your friends what they should do.

Remember to include the e-mail addresses of all your friends.

Send the e-mail.

Next step
- *Try the same activity with e-friends in other countries. You could make your message travel to four different countries and then back to you again!*

Internet Projects for Primary Schools
Using E-mail
© A & C Black 2001

Make up a story

Work with a partner to write a story using e-mail. Plan the story first, using the items and boxes below.

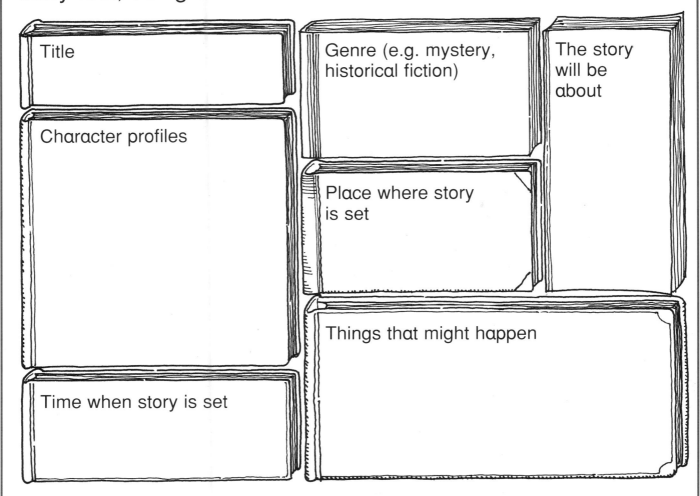

Title

Character profiles

Time when story is set

Genre (e.g. mystery, historical fiction)

The story will be about

Place where story is set

Things that might happen

Now write your story by following the instructions.

1. Decide who will write the first paragraph.
2. Author A chooses a story card and writes a paragraph.
   Go online and send it to Author B.
3. Author B writes the next paragraph beneath
   and sends the message back to Author A.
4. Continue until you finish the story!

On your turn, pick a story card. See if you can include the idea in your paragraph.

Next step
- Print out your completed story.
- With your partner. What can you improve?
- Write a second draft of the story.

Story cards

Cut out the cards.

Danger!	A narrow escape
An argument	A mistaken identity
A theft	A competition
A big disappointment	A storm
Some good news	An accident
A journey	A stranger arrives
A good deed	A lost pet
An old map	A lighthouse
An e-mail message	A valuable ring
A footprint	A kind neighbour
A message from abroad	A funfair
A day out	An injured bird

Internet Projects for Primary Schools
Using E-mail
© A & C Black 2001

A list poem

In a group, you are going to write a list poem using e-mail.

Read this verse from a list poem.

School dinner
Baked potatoes, baked beans,
Sausages, peas.
Treacle tart, rice pud,
Mmm, yes please!

Write ideas for your own list poem about favourite dinners.

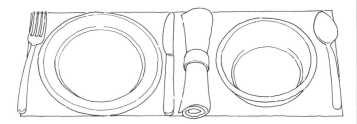

Follow the instructions.

It doesn't have to rhyme.

1. Decide who will write the first verse.
2. If it is you, write your verse offline in an e-mail message. Go online and send it to someone else in your group.
3. The next person writes their verse beneath and sends the poem to someone else.
4. Continue until everyone has written a verse.
5. Edit the poem on screen. Think of a line to finish the poem. It could be a question, such as, 'These are our favourite foods. What are yours?'

Next step
- Copy the finished poem into a word-processing program.
- Check the spelling and punctuation.
- Print out the poem and illustrate it.

Leisure time

You are going to carry out a survey of what pupils at your school do in their free time.

For each activity, write approximately how many hours you spend doing it each week.

Activity	Hours spent doing it each week
Playing sport	
Watching TV	
Reading	
Playing computer games	
Other	

On a computer, make a table like the one above.

Write an e-mail to five pupils in your school. Ask them to fill in the chart and return it. Send the chart as an e-mail attachment.

When you receive the results, work out the total hours spent on each activity.

Playing sport _____ hours   Playing computer games _____ hours

Watching TV _____ hours   Other _____ hours

Reading _____ hours

Next step

- Produce a bar chart to show the results of your survey.
- Which is the most popular leisure activity? Which is the least popular?

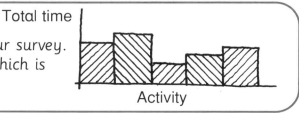

Internet Projects for Primary Schools
Using E-mail
© A & C Black 2001

My journey to school

You are going to e-mail someone from a different area, describing your journey to school. Use this page to make notes. Ask the person to e-mail you details of their journey.

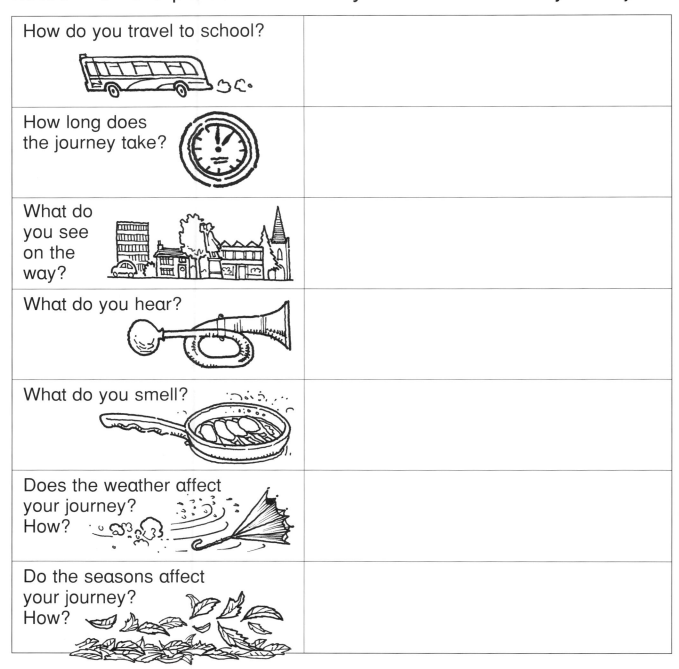

How do you travel to school?	
How long does the journey take?	
What do you see on the way?	
What do you hear?	
What do you smell?	
Does the weather affect your journey? How?	
Do the seasons affect your journey? How?	

Write and send your e-mail.

Check your spelling.

Next step
- Compare your journey with that of the person from a different area.
- Write down similarities and differences between the two journeys.

68

Holiday survey

You are going to carry out a holiday survey. First, write about the last time you went on holiday. Fill in the gaps.

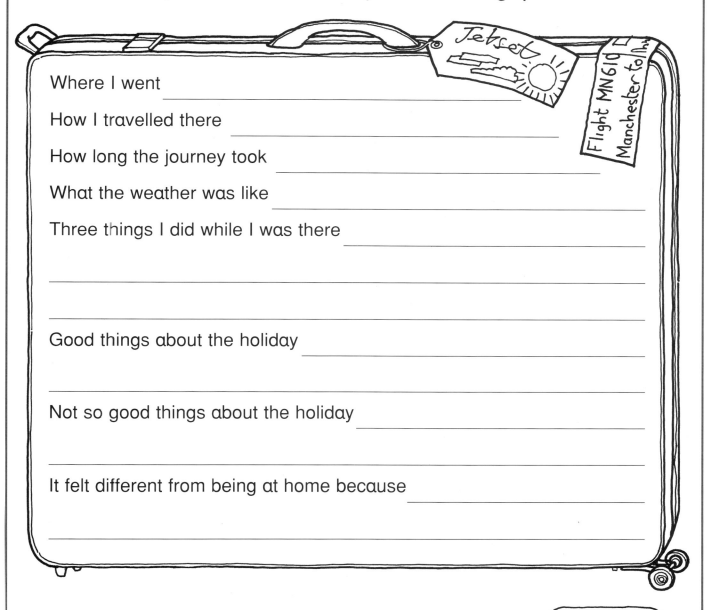

Where I went _____

How I travelled there _____

How long the journey took _____

What the weather was like _____

Three things I did while I was there _____

_____

_____

Good things about the holiday _____

_____

Not so good things about the holiday _____

_____

It felt different from being at home because _____

_____

Use these ideas to help you write an e-mail questionnaire. Ask questions to find out why people go on holiday and where they go.

Check your spelling.

Send your questionnaire to three adults and three children.

Next step
● *Look at the completed questionnaires. On a map, find the places where people have been.*
● *What the three most popular destinations?*

Internet Projects for Primary Schools
Using E-mail
© A & C Black 2001

A legend

You are going to write an e-mail telling a friend about a myth or legend.

Pick one of these, or choose one of your own.

Use books, CD-ROMs or websites.

Rama and Sita   Merlin and King Arthur   Osiris and Isis

Find out about the legend and make notes.

Title

Country it comes from	Names of main characters
Moral of the story	
	What the characters are like (e.g. good or evil, brave or cowardly, wise or foolish)

Write up your notes in an e-mail.

Ask your friend to research a different myth or legend and e-mail you their report.

Check your spelling.

Next step
- Compare the two myths or legends. List any similarities between them.

Think about the characters and the themes.

An invitation

Find out the details of an event that is going to take place at your school, such as a sports event or a car boot sale.

Plan an invitation to send to people outside the school.

Event:

You are invited to

_____

on _____

at _____

At the event, there will be:

Write the name of the event.

Where will it take place?

Write the date and time.

Write what will happen at the event. Make it sound exciting.

If you want to receive a reply, write R.S.V.P. with your name and e-mail address beneath.

Check your spelling.

Write your invitation in an e-mail. Make sure you include all the important details.

Next step
- Design your invitation in a word-processing or DTP program. Insert pictures or the school logo.
- Save the invitation. Send it as an e-mail attachment.

Internet Projects for Primary Schools
Using E-mail
© A & C Black 2001

Career interview

You are going to interview someone by e-mail about their job. Read what these people say about their jobs.

firefighter I wear a uniform and a helmet to stop myself from getting injured.

secretary I work in a busy office.

bank manager The best thing about my job is meeting people.

doctor I enjoy helping others.

Find the e-mail address of someone who does a job you are interested in.

Write some questions you would like to ask the person.

You could choose a vet, a police officer, or someone else.

What time do you usually start work?

Do you enjoy your job?

Write your e-mail. Leave a space for the answer after each question.

Send the e-mail.

Check your spelling.

Next step
● When you receive a reply, use the information to write a report about the job.

72

Healthy eating

You are going to write an information sheet for younger pupils about healthy eating.

Look at the types of food on this diagram.

Use the diagram to help you write your information sheet in an e-mail.

Explain why it is important to eat healthily.

Send the e-mail to younger pupils at your school.

Write in paragraphs and use sub-headings. Check your spelling.

Next step
- Copy your information into a word-processing program. Lay out the text for a display.
- Find clip-art pictures to go with it. Paste them in.
- Print out the sheet.

Internet Projects for Primary Schools
Using E-mail
© A & C Black 2001

Comparing costs

You are going to find out how much things cost in another country. First, fill in the answers to this questionnaire.

Questionnaire

How much do you spend each week on snacks and sweets? _____

How much does your favourite magazine or comic cost? _____

How much does a CD normally cost? _____

How much is the child fare for a short bus journey? _____

How much does your local newspaper cost? _____

How much did your last pair of shoes or trainers cost? _____

How much does it costs to go swimming at the leisure centre? _____

Write the questions in an e-mail.
Send it to an e-pal in another country.

> Use a newspaper or a web site.

Find out the currency exchange rate for that country.

£1 = _____

> Use a calculator if you need to. Round the numbers up or down.

When you receive a reply, change the answers into pounds and pence.

Compare the prices.

Which things are cheaper in the foreign country?

Which things are more expensive?

Next step
● Produce a spreadsheet to show the results of your project.

Internet Projects for Primary Schools
Using E-mail
© A & C Black 2001

Animal habitats: 1

You are going to research a habitat, then use e-mail to exchange information with another school.

With your class, visit a habitat near your school. It might be a wood, a park, a pond or the seaside.

Habitat:_____

Make notes about what the habitat is like.

_____

_____

_____

Word bank

light	dark	sunny
shady	windy	warm
cool	dry	damp
wet		sheltered

List the animals you find. For each one, say where you saw it, for example, in the air or under a stone.

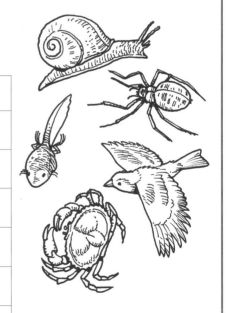

Animal	Where found

Check your spelling.

Next step
● In an e-mail, describe the habitat and the animals you found.
● Send your e-mail to a class in another school and ask the pupils to e-mail you the results of their habitat survey.

Internet Projects for Primary Schools
Using E-mail
© A & C Black 2001

Animal habitats: 2

Look at the information you receive from the other school in the previous activity. Record similarities and differences between the habitats on the chart.

Similarities between _____ and _____	Differences between _____ and _____

What is useful about sharing information with other schools by e-mail?

_____

_____

Did you experience any problems? If so, what?

_____

_____

(Discuss your answers with a friend.)

Next step
● Why do you think animals are found in some places and not in others? Discuss your ideas with a friend.

(Think about what the habitats are like.)

Internet Projects for Primary Schools
Using E-mail
© A & C Black 2001

Maths tips

You are going to swap maths tips with a friend by e-mail.

Read Nabil's maths tip.

> The last digit of any even number is 0, 2, 4, 6 or 8.

(Example) 10, 12, 14, 16 and 18 are all even numbers.

Write your own maths tip. Give examples.

> It could be about adding odd or even numbers.

_____

_____

_____

Read Emily's maths tip.

> To find if a number is a multiple of 9, add up the digits and see if they total 9.

(Example) 18 is a multiple of 9. 1 + 8 = 9
36 is a multiple of 9. 3 + 6 = 9

Write your own maths tip about recognising multiples. Give examples.

> Think about how to recognise multiples of 3, 4 or 5.

_____

_____

_____

Write your maths tips in an e-mail. Ask your friend to send you some more maths tips back. Send the e-mail.

Next step
- When you receive a reply, forward the e-mail to the rest of your group.
- List all the maths tips your group has collected.

Internet Projects for Primary Schools
Using E-mail
© A & C Black 2001

Recycling questionnaire

You need help with planning a project on recycling.

Write a questionnaire to e-mail to other pupils in your school. Use this page to plan what you want to ask.

Recycling questionnaire

Which of these types of rubbish does your home produce?

paper . . .

You might want to find out:

◆ types of rubbish;

◆ whether rubbish is reused or recycled;

◆ how much rubbish is produced (how many bag-fulls;

◆ whether this can be reduced and how.

Word bank

paper   cardboard

drinks cans   bottles

glass   jars

plastic

Write your questions in an e-mail. Leave a space for the answer after each question.

Send your e-mail.

Check your spelling.

Next step
● Using the information from your class research, write a report about how environmentally friendly your school is.
● Include suggestions on how pupils can become more environmentally friendly.
● Publish the report on your school web site.

Ask an expert: 1

If there is something you want to find out, e-mail someone who will know the answer.

Think of something you want to know about your local area.

_____

_____

I want to find a museum that has displays on the Romans.

List people you could e-mail to find out the answer.

_____

_____

_____

Idea bank

TOURIST INFORMATION

Find some e-mail addresses of people who can help you. Write them here.

_____

_____

_____

_____

_____

Look in books, magazines and newspaper articles.

Next step
- Use a search engine to find web sites related to what you want to find out.
- Look on the web sites for e-mail contact addresses.

Internet Projects for Primary Schools
Using E-mail
© A & C Black 2001

Ask an expert: 2

Choose whom you think is the best person to ask.

E-mail address: _____

Why have you chosen this person? _____

_____

_____

Plan what you will write in your e-mail.

My name is

I am

I would like to find out

because

I think you might be able to help because

Tips

◆ Keep it short!

◆ Start by saying who you are and how old you are.

◆ Say what you want to know and why.

◆ Be polite.

Write the e-mail.

Send it.

Check your spelling.

Next step
- Did you receive a reply? If so, how useful was it?
- If you didn't receive a useful reply, try writing another e-mail to someone else.

80

A local walk

You are going to e-mail a friend telling them about buildings near where you live.

On a map of your local area, find two interesting buildings that are near each other.

Names of buildings

1 _____

2 _____

Fill in the chart with what you know about the buildings.

	Building 1	Building 2
When it was built		
What it is used for today		
What it was used for in the past		
Interesting features		

Find out more. Add to or correct your notes.

Write your e-mail.

Use books, leaflets and newspapers.

Next step
- On the map, draw a route in pencil which takes you past the buildings and back to where you started.
- Scan the map into your computer.
- Send your e-mail with the map as an attachment.

Internet Projects for Primary Schools
Using E-mail
© A & C Black 2001

A local hero

You are going to e-mail a friend telling them about a local hero.

Find out about someone from your area who has done something remarkable. It could be someone alive or someone from the past.

Use books, newspapers and libraries.

LOCAL HERO

Name:

When and where born:

Age/when died:

Where lives/lived:

Job:

Special achievements:

Why I think this person deserves to be remembered:

Use your notes to write a short biography of the person.

Send it to a friend in an e-mail.

A biography tells the story of someone else's life.

Next step
- Draw a time-line of the most important events in your life.
- Use the time-line to help you write your autobiography.
- E-mail it to a friend.

Music review

You are going to e-mail a music review to a friend.

Go to one of these web sites.

www.nme.com   www.dotmusic.com

Circle the one you choose.

Find a sound file of a piece of music you like. Download it on to your hard disk.

Write about the piece of music on the chart.

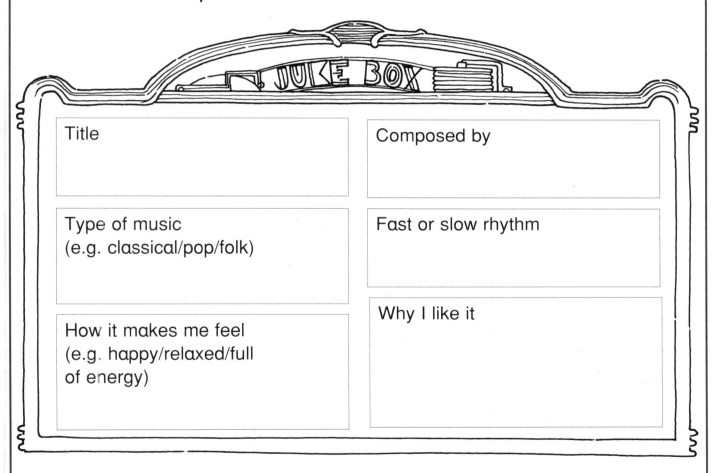

Title	Composed by
Type of music (e.g. classical/pop/folk)	Fast or slow rhythm
How it makes me feel (e.g. happy/relaxed/full of energy)	Why I like it

Write up your notes as an e-mail review.

Send your e-mail to a friend with the sound file as an attachment.

Next step
- *Swap e-mails with a friend.*
- *Listen to the piece of music and read the review.*
- *Write a reply saying why you do or do not share your friend's opinion.*

83

Life in another country

Write a questionnaire to send to pupils in another country.
Use this page to plan what you want to ask.

Lifestyle questionnaire

You might want to find out:

what their school is like

what subjects they learn

what their homes are like

what their town or village is like

what music they listen to

what religion they are (if any)

what they do in their free time

Write your questions in an e-mail. Leave a
space for the answer after each question.

Send your e-mail.

Next step
- Write an e-mail about yourself and where you live. Use the questions to help you.
- Find photos of your local area and scan them into your computer.
- Find a sound file of music that you like.
- Send your e-mail to pupils in another country,
  with the photos and sound files as attachments.

Try typing the name of your town
or area into a search engine.

Internet Projects for Primary Schools
Using E-mail
© A & C Black 2001

Abbreviations

Some people use short-cuts, or abbreviations, so that their messages are quicker to type.

Look at these abbreviations of phrases.

They are made up of the first letter of each word.

BTW	by the way	FC	fingers crossed
POV	point of view	NRN	no reply necessary

Think of some phrases you use. Write abbreviations for them.

_____

_____

_____

Look at these abbreviations of words.

Say them out loud.

2day today	B4 before	L8 late

Make up abbreviations for these words.

tonight _____ forget _____

great _____ into _____

wonder_____ hand_____

Look for the 'and' symbol.

Next step
- Make up some more abbreviations of your own.
- Write an e-mail to a friend. Use some of the abbreviations.
- Does your friend understand them?

Internet Projects for Primary Schools
Using E-mail
© A & C Black 2001

Smileys

These pictures are called smileys. You can use them in e-mails to show when you are joking, or whether you are happy or sad.

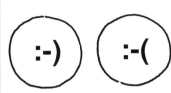

Look at the pictures sideways! They are made using letters and punctuation keys.

Write what you think these smileys mean.

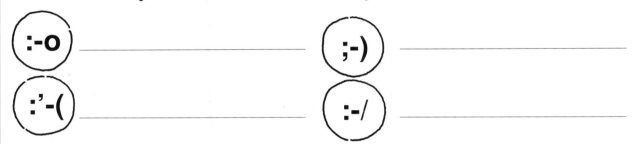

Try copying the smileys using a computer keyboard.

Use the keyboard to make up smileys for these. Sketch them here.

Try using
P D d &

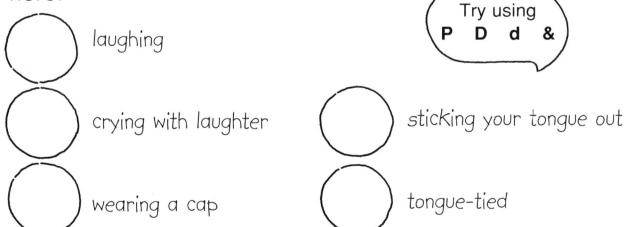

laughing

crying with laughter   sticking your tongue out

wearing a cap   tongue-tied

Can you make up more smileys of your own?

Next step
- Write an e-mail to a friend. You could tell the story of a day out or something interesting that has happened to you.
- Use smileys in between the sentences to show how you felt.

Signing off

Look at these ways of signing off an e-mail.

The pictures are made using letters and punctuation keys.

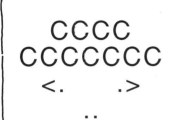 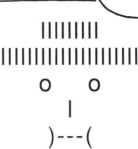

```
CCCC          C           IIIIIIIII
CCCCCCC       U        IIIIIIIIIIIIIIIIII
<.     .>   L8TER         o     o
    ..                        I
    Ö                      )---(
```

Try copying the signatures using a computer keyboard.

Make up your own signatures. Try one that uses words and one that uses a picture.

First, draw sketches of what you want them to look like.

Don't make them too complicated!

Now practise making your signatures using a computer keyboard.

Next step
- Write a short e-mail to a friend.
- Type a signature at the end of the message.
- Send the message.

Internet Projects for Primary Schools
Using E-mail
© A & C Black 2001

87

RECOMMENDED WEB SITES

In this section you will find addresses of recommended web sites the authors have used personally and in training sessions with teachers. Each URL is for a website's home page. You may have to click a further link or more to find exactly what you want.

Most good web sites provide a direct e-mail link so that you can quickly contact them. Once the link is clicked, it will open *Outlook Express* in the usual way and will present you with a new e-mail screen into which to type your message.

> **HINTS AND TIPS**
>
> If the Internet is very busy, you may hit a 'traffic jam'. A web site may go off-line briefly to be updated.
>
> Look in educational magazines and newspaper supplements for more web site recommendations.

Category	Type	URL	Notes
Books			
These sites provide the basis for reading lists, learning about authors and book publishing.			
	The Book Trust	www.booktrust.org.uk	
	Children's Literature	www.acs.ucalgary.ca	
	Scottish Book Trust	www.scottishbooktrust.com	
Downloads			
If your school service provider does not regularly upgrade your software, or if you work from home, here are the web sites from which you can download upgrades at no cost.			
	Internet Explorer®	www.microsoft.com/windows	Browsers upgrades and add-ons
	Netscape®	www.netscape.com	The other main browser
	Shareware	www.shareware.com	Links to other download sites
Educational			
Useful sites for general use of computers in the classroom.			
	Beginner's Centre	www.northernwebs.com/bc	A user's guide to the Internet
	Eduweb/Learning Alive	www.eduweb.co.uk, www.learningalive.co.uk	Research Machine's gateway site
	Microsoft	www.microsoft.com/education	Classroom resources
	Becta	www.becta.org.uk/index.html	
Experts			
	Pitsco	www.askanexpert.com	Where children can 'ask the expert'
Government strategies, curricula and qualifications			
Official sites for details of the national curriculum, schemes of work and standards.			
	Curriculum 2000	www.curriculum2000.co.uk	Curriculum 2000 for UK schools
	DfEE	www.dfee.gov.uk	Department of Education
	National Curriculum	www.nc.uk.net	National Curriculum online
	Standards	www.standards.dfee.gov.uk	Literacy/Numeracy/Schemes
	VTC – England	www.vtc.ngfl.gov.uk	Virtual Teachers Centre: England
	VTC – Scotland VTC	www.svtc.org.uk	Virtual Teachers Centre: Scotland
	VTC – Cymru	www.vtccymru.ngfl.wales.gov.uk	Virtual Teachers Centre: Cymru
IAP			
	Information on . . .	www.thedirectory.org	Addresses of access providers

Museums

A selection of sites that allow you to view collections of works of art, historical items and natural history. Some of the sites allow you to tour the museum, and many of them provide excellent reference material you can download.

British Museum	www.thebritishmuseum.ac.uk	The British Museum, London
Hermitage	www.hermitagemuseum.org	State Museum, St Petersburg
Imperial War	www.iwm.org.uk	Gateway to other wartime life sites
Metropolitan	www.metmuseum.org	Metropolitan Museum of New York
MoMI	www.bfi.org.uk	Museum of the Moving Image
Musée d'Orsay	www.musee-orsay.fr	Musée d'Orsay, Paris
Natural History	www.nhm.ac.uk	London's fabulous museum
NMPFT	www.nmpft.org.uk	National Museum of Photography, Film & TV
National Gallery	www.nationalgallery.org.uk	The National Gallery, London
National Railway	www.nrm.org.uk	National Railway Museum
Natural History	www.ology.amnh.org	American site with dinosaur activities
Science Museum	www.nmsi.ac.uk	Gateway leading to other museums
The Tate Museum	www.tate.org.uk	Links to other sites – Tate Modern

Newspapers

The Guardian	www.guardian.co.uk	UK newspaper
Independent	www.independent.co.uk	UK newspaper
New York Times	www.nytimes.com	US newspaper
Washington Post	www.washingtonpost.com	US newspaper

Parents

These sites offer additional resources that you may need for special downloads (plug-ins) to function properly.

DfEE Parents Centre	www.parents.dfee.gov.uk	Information and links
Schoolzone	www.schoolzone.co.uk	Information and links

Plug-ins

Quicktime™	www.apple.com	Used to play video clips
RealPlayer®	www.real.com	For on-line stores and radio stations
Shockwave®	www.macromedia.com	To display 'Flash' animations properly
	www.timecast.com	Real Audio sites and live concerts

Qualifications

Sites offering educational resources.

OCR	www.ocr.org.uk	Oxford, Cambridge & RSA

Reference and Resources

Aesop's Fables	www.umass.edu/aesop/contents.html	Texts to download and use
Dorling Kindersley	www.dk.com	CD-ROMs and books
Encarta	www.encarta.msn.com	Packed with multimedia
Oxford ED	www.oed.com	Standard Oxford Dictionary
PastPix	www.pastpix.com	Pictures to simulate
Primary Resources	www.primaryresources.co.uk	Classroom resources
Project Gutenberg	www.promo.net	Free downloads of classic texts
Teacher Resource Exchange	www.contribute.ngfl.gov.uk	Exchange of teachers' work
Wacky Web Tales	www.eduplace.com/tales/index.html	Fun stories for classroom use

Safety issues

Superhighway Safety	www.epals.com	
	www.safety.ngfl.gov.uk	

Science

NASA homepage	www.nasa.gov	Earth and space science resources
The Meteorological Office	www.met-office.gov.uk/education/	Weather reports, maps, information
Yorkshire Electricity	www.yeg.co.uk/fun/	All about electricity for children

89

SEARCH ENGINES

Directories and indexes for starting keyword searches.

Alta Vista®	www.altavista.com	
AskJeeves™	www.ask.com	Question-based
Ask Jeeves for kids	www.ajkids.com	Question-based kids search
Excite	www.excite.co.uk	Uk-based general search
Google®	www.google.com	
HotBot®	www.hotbot.com	
Lycos®	www.lycos.com	
Magellan	www.magellan.excite.com	Popular web Directory
Mirago	www.mirago.co.uk	Uk-based general search
UK Plus	www.ukplus.co.uk	Uk-based general search
Yahoo UK/Ireland®	www.yahoo.co.uk	Uk-based general search
Yahooligans	www.yahooligans.com	Yahoo's kids search

Software

Websites from where software can be downloaded.

Becta Software	www.besd.becta.org.uk	
Compression	www.winzip.com	Winzip® for Windows
Shared	www.shareware.com	Software on a shared basis
Softease	www.textease.com	DTP, Database, Spreadsheet package

Special Needs

These sites offer advice and resources for SEN.

DfEE ICT support	www.dfee.gov.uk/sen	SEN links etc.
NASEN	www.nasen.org.uk	National Association for Special Educational Needs
BDA	www.bda-dyslexia.org.uk	British Dyslexia Association
RNIB	www.rnib.org.uk	Royal National Institute for the Blind
NAGC	www.rmplc.co.uk/orgs/nagc	National Association for Gifted Children

Teachers

Web sites offering a range of cross-curricular ideas and resources.

AskJeeves for . . .	www.ajschools.com/teachers	Useful resources & ideas
BBC Education	www.bbc.co.uk/education/schools	Home page with numerous links
Click Teaching	www.clickteaching.com	Useful resources and ideas
Educate the Children	www.educate.org.uk/teacher_zone	Useful ideas and information
ICTteachers	www.icteachers.co.uk/	Useful resources and ideas
ICT toolbox	http://crduk.extra.bt.com/ict/toolbox	BTs school resources site
Kent LEA	www.kented.org.uk/ngfl	LEA site with ideas and resources
Northern Grid	www.northerngrid.org	Northern LEA Consortium
Schoolzone	www.schoolzone.co.uk	Ideas & Information for teachers and parents
School Express	www.freeworksheets.com	American site with free worksheets
Spot Pages	www.freenetpages.co.uk	Key Stage1 resources and ideas
Stockport LEA	www.stockportmbc.gov.uk	LEA site with ideas and resources
Sunshine Online	www.literacyhour.co.uk/index.html	Simple ideas for lessons
Teacher Net	www.teachernet.gov.uk	
Teaching Ideas	www.teachingideas.co.uk	Ideas and resources including ICT
VTC – England	www.timeplan.com	Virtual Teachers Centre – England
VTC – Scotland	www.svtc.org.uk	Virtual Teachers Centre – Scotland
VTC – Cymru	www.vtccymru.ngfl.wales.gov.uk	Virtual Teachers Centre – Wales
Welcome to the web	www.teachingideas.co.uk	Excellent Internet activities

TV news

BBC	www.bbc.co.uk	Home page with numerous links
ITN	www.itn.co.uk	British network
CNN	www.cnn.com	American network
Virgin Radio	www. virginradio.co.uk	

SECTION 6:
AT-A-GLANCE GUIDES

This section contains a basic checklist of computer skills and an explanation of jargon words used in this book. You may find it useful to make copies of pages 91 to 93 for posting in the classroom, computer room or at home.

What basic skills do I need?

Your PC
- [ ] Turn on and start up the computer
- [ ] Know your way around the keyboard
- [ ] Load and use a floppy disk, CD-ROM
- [ ] Turn on and set up a printer

Mouse Skills
- [ ] Use a mouse to select icons
- [ ] Use a mouse to drag and drop objects
- [ ] Use a mouse to open and close windows
- [ ] Single-click and double-click to open applications (programs)

The Task Bar
- [ ] Find the task bar on the desktop
- [ ] Use the task bar to run more than one program and switch between programs
- [ ] Click on the system tray on the task bar

The Start Button
- [ ] Click on the *Start* button on the task bar to open the *Start* menu
- [ ] Launch programs from the *Start* menu
- [ ] Use the *Start* menu to shut down

Desktop Icons
- [ ] Double-click on an icon to start a program
- [ ] Drag and drop icons around the desktop and rearrange them to tidy the desktop
- [ ] Double-click on an icon to open another window

Desktop Windows
- [ ] Move a window by dragging on the title bar
- [ ] Use the *Close* button
- [ ] Use the *Minimise* and *Restore* buttons
- [ ] Restore a window from the task bar

Disks, Folders, Files
- [ ] Name and save a file on to the hard drive
- [ ] Transfer work from a floppy disk
- [ ] Choose a file from a folder

Internet Projects for Primary Schools
Using E-mail
© A & C Black 2001

Disks, Folders, Files (continued)	☐ Create and name a folder
	☐ Click on a drive to see the files and folders
	☐ Save work in appropriately named files
	☐ Retrieve saved files from folders
	☐ Add, change and re-save a file
Information Backup	☐ Establish a routine of backing up work
	☐ Copy files on to floppy disks
	☐ Store back-up disks in a safe place
My Computer	☐ Find the *My Computer* icon
	☐ Double-click on the *My Computer* icon to look at the drives
	☐ Double-click to look at the *Control Panel*
	☐ Close the *My Computer* window
The Recycle Bin	☐ Delete an old work file in the *My Computer* window
	☐ Double-click on the *Recycle Bin* to see what is stored there temporarily
	☐ Restore a file held in the *Recycle Bin*
	☐ Permanently delete a file
Control Panel	☐ Find and launch the *Control Panel* window from the *Start* menu
	☐ Select the mouse icon in the *Control Panel* to change its speed
	☐ Close the *Control Panel* window
Printers	☐ Check the printer is on and ready to use
	☐ Use the *Print Preview* option
	☐ Use the *Quick Print* button
	☐ Print out more than one copy using the *Print* dialogue boxes
	☐ Choose one page from a longer document to print out
E-mail and the Internet	☐ Log on to the Internet
	☐ Send an e-mail
	☐ Read an e-mail from your inbox
	☐ Store an e-mail address in the address book
	☐ Visit a web site by entering its address
	☐ Bookmark a web site to explore later
	☐ Log off from the Internet

IT PAYS TO PRACTISE:

- Mouse skills such as clicking and dragging
- Navigating the desktop and knowing where to find:
  ▲ the floppy disk drive
  ▲ CD-ROM drive
  ▲ *My Computer*
  ▲ *My Documents*
  ▲ *My Briefcase*
  ▲ the *Recycle Bin*
  ▲ the applications
- Handling windows:
  ▲ dragging
  ▲ re-sizing/minimising
  ▲ scrolling
  ▲ closing down
- Routine 'housekeeping' – creating a useful filing system with folders and files organised systematically. Using e-mail, create folders for incoming and outgoing mail to fellow teachers, pupils, your headteacher and the LEA.
- Saving across a network and backing up files as a regular precaution
- Loading a printer with paper, clearing paper jams and changing ink cartridges.

HINTS AND TIPS

When using 'Outlook Express' , you can set up the system so that the address to which you are sending a message is automatically added to your address book. Click on 'Tools-Options', and on the 'Send' tab click 'Automatically put people reply to in my address book'.

92

Internet Projects for Primary Schools
Using E-mail
© A & C Black 2001

GLOSSARY

access provider A company that lets you connect to the Internet by dialling into their computer. *See also* Internet Service Provider.

address On the Internet, the precise location of a particular web site or web page, that is also known as its URL. *See also* URL.

ADSL Short for 'asymmetric digital subscriber line'. A high-speed permanent connection to the Internet. *See also* ISDN.

animated GIF Two or more image files combined to create a very simple moving picture or animation. *See also* GIF.

application A software program designed to let you do particular kinds of task on your computer. A word-processing application, for example, is designed for working on screen with words but no pictures.

back-ups Copies of computer files kept on storage disks, not your hard disk. It is vital to make and keep back-ups in case files are lost or corrupted. *See also* floppy disk.

bandwidth Measurement of the amount of information that can be transferred over an Internet telephone connection.

bin An area on your hard disk where deleted files stay until a decision is made to get rid of them. On an Apple Macintosh computer the bin is called the Wastebasket.

bookmarks *Netscape Navigator*'s way of storing direct links to the addresses of favourite web sites. See also '*Favorites*'.

browser The vital piece of Internet software for viewing pages from the World Wide Web. The two most popular browsers are *Internet Explorer* and *Netscape Navigator*.

cache A folder on your hard drive in which your browser stores all the files it downloads from the World Wide Web (in case you want to view those pages again).

CD-ROM Short for 'compact disc, read-only memory'. Used for games, information and software installation, this sort of compact disc cannot be recorded over (hence 'read-only').

clip art Images that have been created by someone else for you to use on computer.

clipboard An area on your hard disk where anything you copy or cut from a file is temporarily stored until it is pasted into another file (or another place in the same file).

cookie A small text file that some web sites store on your computer so that they know who you are next time you visit.

copy, cut, paste A set of really useful editing tools found within many kinds of programs including word processors and browsers.

copyright Laws that protect text and images from unlawful copying.

cyberspace A word coined by William Gibson in his novel *Necromancer*. It is used as a very generalised term for the Internet and everything that comes with it.

Data Protection Act Act of law designed to protect individuals from misuse of information held on computer or file about them. Find out more about it from: **http://www.open. gov.uk/dpr/dprhome.htm.**

database A collection of stored records which might include text, images and/or numbers.

digital camera A camera that does not use photographic film that needs processing, but instead captures and stores images as digital files. These files can be transferred on to your computer for display, printing out, sending in an e-mail attachment or posting on a web page.

domain name The unique name given to every web site on the Internet such as: **www.sitetraining.com**

download To copy computer data from one computer to another (or to a disk), possibly via the Internet. The opposite term is uploading.

drag, drop Moving icons, text or objects around on screen. To drag something, click the mouse button over it and move the mouse with the button held down. Drop the object in the right place by releasing the mouse button.

DTP Short for 'desktop publishing'. Describes applications that combine word-processing functions with image-handling functions.

export To send data from one computer program to another. For example, you can export an image that you have found on the Internet in a format that you could use in a DTP program.

FAQ Short for 'frequently-asked questions'. These – along with their answers – are often displayed on a web site or in a newsgroup.

favorites A menu in Microsoft's *Internet Explorer* browser (and a corresponding folder on your hard disk) that contains shortcuts to web sites that you visit regularly. *See also* Bookmarks.

93

file format The type of file. For example, a JPEG is a file format that is suitable for images, whereas Text Only is one format suitable for words.

file management Organising your computer files according to a sensible, user-friendly system. This is especially important when the use of a computer is shared.

floppy disk A storage device on which you can back up small files (usually up to 1.44 Mb). Despite its name, a floppy disk is square and hard – the round, floppy bit is hidden inside.

font A style of lettering, for example **bold,** *italic* or roman.

freeware Software that you do not have to pay for.

gateway A program or device that acts as a kind of translator between two networks so that they can communicate with each other.

GIF Short for 'graphic interchange format'. One of the two most common file formats for graphics used on the Internet. *See also* JPEG.

graphics General term describing images created and stored on computers.

graphing program A program that will create charts and graphs from the data entered.

history list A list stored by your browser showing recently visited web sites so that you can see where you have been and revisit sites easily.

home page (1) The page displayed by your browser when you start it up, or when you click the *Home* button. (2) The first page (or main contents page) of a web site.

host A computer connected directly to the Internet, usually all the time, such as your Internet Service Provider's computer. The host machine allows other computers to connect to it.

housekeeping Regular computer system maintenance such as deleting out-of-date files, organising files into directories or folders, making back-up copies of files and emptying the Recycle Bin.

HTML Short for 'hypertext mark-up language'. The computer code used to create web pages and links.

http Short for 'hypertext transport protocol'. Often forms the beginning of a web site address or URL.

icon A small picture on screen that represents a function, program, file or folder. You can click on an icon to jump to a different place or to perform a task.

ICT Short for 'Information and Communication Technology', now one of the core subjects of the National Curriculum.

image map A single image divided into several 'hot' areas and placed on a web page. Each area will take you to a different page or file when clicked.

import To receive some computer data from another program or storage device.

Internet A gigantic network of computers, all linked together and able to exchange information, that no one completely owns or controls. Sometimes, its name is shortened to 'the Net'.

Internet Explorer The name of Microsoft's browser software. *See also* Browser.

Internet Service Provider (ISP) A company that allows you to connect to the Internet by dialling into their host machine. *See also* host.

Intranet A network of computers that are linked together using Internet technology, but which are private and not accessible to everyone. Many educational institutions have an Intranet.

ISDN Short for 'integrated services digital network'. A kind of telephone line that can handle (transport) lots of complex data, including large images, very speedily.

JPEG Short for 'joint photographic experts group'. One of the two most common file formats for pictures used on the Internet. *See also* GIF.

keyword, key phrase A word or phrase that you type into a search engine, so that it can look for any web sites that may contain information relevant to that word or phrase.

log off To disconnect from the Internet, so that your browser breaks the link with the host computer.

log on To connect to the Internet, by telling your browser to dial up and form a link with the host computer. Often, you have to identify yourself at the start of a session, by typing in a username and password. *See also* username.

menu The list of possible options in a program.

mirror site An exact copy of a web site, located on a different computer.

modem A device that that allows a computer to send and receive digital information down analogue phone lines. It may be inside or outside the computer.

multimedia A mix of differently formatted information, such as text, still images, sound files and animation, such as those stored on a CD-ROM.

netiquette Term used to describe accepted rules of behaviour on the Internet (formed from 'Net' and 'etiquette'). An example of bad netiquette is typing e-mails in capital letters, which looks like you are shouting.

network Two or more computers that are connected to each other by cables, or that can be connected to each other via modems and telephone lines, so that they can swap data.

newsgroup A group of Internet users that swap ideas and opinions on a shared, common interest.

offline Not connected to the Internet but able to continue working on files. *See also* online.

online Connected to the Internet. *See also* offline.

portal An Internet site that has a search engine and a directory of links to other websites. Portals make good starting points for Internet searches.

QCA Short for 'Qualifications and Curriculum Authority'.

qwerty Description of the traditional keyboard arrangement, as on a typewriter's keys: the letters 'q', 'w', 'e', 'r', 't' and 'y' are the first letter keys to appear at the top left.

RAM Short for 'random access memory'. Short-term memory used by your computer.

refresh, reload Forcing the browser to download a web page again by clicking a tool bar button labelled *Refresh* (in *Internet Explorer*) or *Reload* (in *Netscape Navigator*). This can be useful if the page seems to have 'frozen'.

ROM Short for 'read-only memory'. A way of storing information so that it can be read very fast, but not changed in any way, for example on a CD-ROM. *See also* CD-ROM.

search engine A website that maintains an index of other web pages and sites, allowing you to search for pages on a particular subject by entering keywords or key phrases. Examples include *Yahoo* and *Google*.

server A computer that provides a service, such as hosting many web sites, or connecting to your service provider's mail server when you decide to send or receive e-mail.

service provider A company that gives you access to the Internet by letting you dial in to their computer. This may be an Internet Service Provider or an online service.

URL Short for 'uniform resource locator'. The unique address of a website or web page.

username The unique name that you use when using your computer in order to identify yourself.

virus A piece of computer code that can attach itself to programs or files on your computer and corrupt or delete them. To avoid 'catching' a virus, check any new files you download using anti-virus software.

WAP Short for 'wireless application protocol'. Describes web-like pages written in a language called WML (similar to HTML) that can be downloaded into WAP-enabled mobile phones and pagers.

web page A single document (usually with **.htm** or **.html** at the end of its name) that is a tiny part of the Internet. Web pages may contain text, images and links to other web pages.

web server A computer or program dedicated to storing Web pages and transmitting them to your computer to be viewed in your browser.

web site A collection of related web pages and files, usually created by or belonging to a single individual or company, and located on the same web server.

word bank A list of words, phrases and pictures that children can click on, rather than typing in the words for themselves. Word banks can be created in some educational software, such as *Textease*, and cut down on errors due to mispellings.

word processor A computer program that allows the user to input text and edit it.

World Wide Web A vast collection of documents and files stored on web servers. The documents are known as web pages and are created using a language called HTML. All these pages and files are linked together by a common language called hypertext.

www Short for 'World Wide Web'. Often found at the beginning of a web address or URL.

INDEX

account, setting up 24
address 8, 9, 20, 22, 29, 34, 35–38, 39, 47, 50, 61 *See also* address book, contacts
address book 14, 16, 17, 29, 30, 31, 36, 38, 39
attachments 17, 19, 42–43, 47

carbon copies 34, 35, 39
CD-ROMs 12, 14, 18, 20, 24, 26
chat lists 15
chat rooms 18, 44
computer equipment 8, 15, 16, 17, 20, 25–27, 46, 48
computer skills 91–92
connecting up 9, 18 *See also* Internet Service Provider, modem
contacts 30, 36–38
costs 7, 18, 20, 34

databases 12, 14
desktop 25, 26, 28, 29
desktop publishing 12, 13
digital cameras 14, 20
domain name 8, 35

e-mail
address 8, 9, 20, 22, 29, 34, 35–38, 39, 47, 50, 61
benefits of 7, 10
definition of 7
educational uses 12–15, 53–55
deleting 31
displaying 33
printing 31, 33
forwarding 31, 39
how it works 8, 16–17
managing 40–41 *See also* folders and sub-folders
opening and reading 30, 31, 32–33
replying to 39
saving 41
sending 30, 31, 39, 42, 50
subject of 33, 34, 35

types of 16
viewing 30, 31
web-based 16, 17, 19, 24
writing 34, 35, 39 *See also* photocopiable activity sheets
emoticons 34, 86, 87
'ePals' 17, 18, 19, 44

filtered/monitored access 19
folders and sub-folders 25, 26, 28, 30, 40–41

hard disk 20
'Hotmail' 17, 24 *See also* e-mail: webmail

icons 21, 24, 25, 27, 28, 43
images 10, 12, 22, 42, 47
inbox 16, 17, 31, 32, 33, 36
Information and Communications Technology (ICT) 11, 12, 13, 14, 24,48
information, exchanging and sharing 10, 13, 14, 21–22, 44 *See also* photocopiable activity sheets
Internet 7, 8, 9–13, 14, 15, 16, 18, 19, 21–22, 28, 46
'Internet Explorer' 29 *See also* software
Internet Service Provider (ISP) 8, 9, 16, 18, 19, 20, 24, 48, 49

mailbox 7, 8
menus 29, 30, 32, 37, 40
mobile phones 7, 10
modem 8, 9, 20, 47
mouse 21, 26, 27
multimedia 10, 12

National Curriculum 11–13, 88 See also Information and Communications Technology
'Netscape Navigator' 29

networks 9, 16, 20, 21, 24, 27, 36
newsgroups 44

online/offline 32, 34
outbox 16, 17, 31, 34
'Outlook Express' 26, 27–33, 36, 38, 44, 46 *See also* software

panels/bars, window 25, 26, 30, 31, 36, 43
password 16, 17, 20, 24, 27, 47
photocopiable activity sheets 56–87
preview panel 30, 33, 43
printer 20, 33, 48

scanners 14, 20
scrolling 26, 33
security 49, 51, 89
servers 8, 9, 16, 51
short-cuts 25, 26
software/programs 8, 16, 18, 20, 24, 25, 27, 28, 46, 47, 48, 90 *See also* 'Outlook Express'

teacher training 15 *See also* Information and Communications Technology, National Curriculum
telephone line 7, 8, 9, 18, 24, 46, 48
text 10, 12 *See also* multimedia, word-processing
text messaging 7
toolbar 30–31, 32

user name 8, 16, 24, 27, 35, 47

video 10, 42, 47
viruses 43, 46, 49

web sites 7, 9, 14, 17, 19, 35, 88–90
word-processing 18, 39, 62

Printed and bound in Great Britain